THE WORLD OF
NORM
MAY NEED REBOOTING

ORCHARD BOOKS
338 Euston Road, London NW1 3BH
Orchard Books Australia
Level 17/207 Kent Street, Sydney, NSW 2000

First published in 2014 by Orchard Books

A Paperback Original

ISBN 978 1 40832 949 8

Text © Jonathan Meres 2014
Illustrations © Donough O'Malley 2014

The rights of Jonathan Meres to be identified as the author and Donough O'Malley to be identified as the illustrator of this work have been asserted by them in accordance with the Copyright, Designs and Patents Act, 1988.

A CIP catalogue record for this book is available from the British Library.

9 10 8

Printed in Great Britain

Orchard Books is a division of Hachette Children's Books, an Hachette UK company.

www.hachette.co.uk

JONATHAN MERES

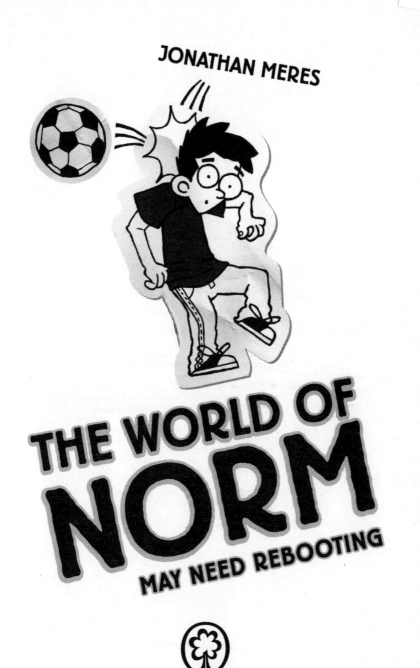

THE WORLD OF
NORM
MAY NEED REBOOTING

ORCHARD

CHAPTER 1

Norm knew it was going to be one of those days when he woke up and found himself in the middle of The French Revolution.

"Norman?" said a strangely familiar-sounding voice.

Uh? thought Norm groggily. What was going on?

Had he fallen asleep in front of the telly? And if so, where was the flipping remote control? Because there **had** to be something better on than **this!**

"You haven't been **asleep**, have you?" said the voice.

There was a burst of laughter. Norm looked around to see a sea of grinning faces looking back at him. Suddenly he knew **exactly** what was going on. He **had** fallen asleep. But **not** in front of the telly. He'd fallen asleep in **class!** No flipping wonder the voice had sounded strangely familiar. It was the voice of his history teacher, Miss Rogers!

"Late night, was it, Norman?"

"What?" yawned Norm.

"Pardon," said Miss Rogers.

"What?" said Norm.

"***Pardon!***" said Miss Rogers. "Not ***what!***"

"Oh, right. Sorry," said Norm.

"Late night, was it?"

"Erm, yeah, kind of," said Norm.

"Good," said Miss Rogers. "Pleased to hear it."

Norm was getting more confused by the second. And he'd been pretty confused in the ***first*** place. "What? I mean, pardon?"

"Well I'd hate to think you'd dropped off because of my ***teaching***."

"No, no, course not, Miss Rogers," said Norm quickly.

There was more laughter. As it happened though, the night before had been a late night – most of which Norm had spent Googling around for potential new bikes, what with his current bike being totally past its ride-by date. How was he *ever* supposed to become World Mountain Biking Champion on an ancient wreck like *that?* Not that there was the *remotest* possibility of his skinflint parents buying him another one. Not until his dad got a job and his mum started working more than five minutes a week at the flipping cake shop there wasn't, anyway. And even then they'd probably want to blow all their money on flipping food and clothes and electricity and stuff, claiming that that was somehow more *important.* It was *so* unfair.

"What were you doing?" said Miss Rogers.

Norm shrugged. "Just thinking."

"I meant what were you doing last night?" said Miss Rogers. "Or don't I want to know?"

Norm thought for a moment. How did **he** know whether his teacher wanted to know what he'd been doing last night or not? What was he? Psychic or something?

"Well, Norman?"

"Looking at bikes," muttered Norm.

"Geek," laughed a voice from the back.

Norm turned around to see Connor Wright, the captain of the football team, smirking at him.

"What was that?" said Norm.

"Er, nothing," said Connor Wright.

"There's nothing geeky about looking at bikes!" spat Norm.

"Whatever," said Connor Wright.

"Better than flipping **football**," muttered Norm.

"You reckon?"

"Yeah, I do actually," said Norm.

"Just 'cos you're rubbish at football," sniggered Connor Wright.

"I'm not rubbish," said Norm. "I'm really good."

"Oh yeah?"

"Yeah," said Norm. "I just don't play, that's all."

"That's quite enough, you two," said Miss Rogers.

Norm sighed. He knew that Connor Wright was right. He really **was** rubbish at football. But Connor Wright wasn't **completely** right. The real reason Norm chose not to play football was that Norm hated football more than just about anything. Well, apart from going for walks. And living in a stupid little house with paper-thin walls and only one toilet. And most vegetables. But apart from that, Norm hated football more than just about anything.

"Open your homework diary please."

Diary? thought Norm. Not *diaries?* He must have misheard. He glanced around the rest of the class. But no one else had made a move.

"Well, Norman?" said Miss Rogers.

Norm pulled a face. "Just me?"

Miss Rogers nodded. "Just you."

"But..."

"I don't see anyone *else* asleep, do you?"

"Give them a few more minutes," mumbled Norm under his breath.

"Oh, dear. That's unfortunate," said Miss Rogers.

"What is?" said Norm.

"Well, that's just doubled the size of your punishment exercise."

Norm heard the words, but it was several seconds before he fully comprehended what they actually meant.

"Punishment exercise?"

"Well, of course," said Miss Rogers. "What do you expect?"

Norm opened his mouth to say something – but suddenly thought better of it and closed it again. Miss Rogers clearly wasn't going to change her mind now. Things weren't about to get any better. They could only get worse. Same as flipping usual.

CHAPTER 2

"You fell **asleep?**" said Mikey in utter disbelief.

"Yes, I fell asleep, Mikey," said Norm.

"You actually fell **asleep?**"

Norm sighed. "Yes, Mikey. I actually fell asleep."

"In **history?**" said Mikey as if that was somehow worse than falling asleep in maths, or geography.

"Yes, Mikey," said Norm, beginning to get more and more exasperated. "In history."

"Whoa," said Mikey.

Gordon flipping Bennet, thought Norm. The way Mikey was going on anybody would think he'd got changed into his flipping pyjamas first – not just accidentally nodded off for a few seconds.

"I didn't **mean** to, Mikey!"

"Well I should hope not," said Mikey.

Norm looked at his best friend. "Have you never fallen asleep, then?"

Mikey looked puzzled. "In school, you mean?"

Norm sighed again. "No, I mean have you ever just generally fallen asleep?"

"What?"

"Of **course** I mean in flipping school, you doughnut!"

"Oh, right," said Mikey. "Erm, no, I don't think so."

Course not, thought Norm. Silly question really. Mikey would **never** do a thing like that, would he? He'd be too busy sticking his hand up and getting every single question right! Just like he used to in primary school. Of course it wasn't Mikey's fault that he was just that little bit better at everything than Norm was. Norm knew that. It was still flipping annoying though. The only consolation, as far as Norm was concerned, was that he and Mikey weren't actually in the same class very often now that they were in secondary school. They were in different classes for nearly all subjects. In fact some days the only time they actually saw each other was at lunch when they walked round the playing field together, chatting. Which was exactly what they were doing now.

"How come?" said Mikey eventually.

"How come what?" said Norm.

"You fell asleep."

Norm looked at Mikey again. For someone who

was supposed to be reasonably intelligent, he didn't half ask some stupid questions sometimes.

"How come I fell **asleep?**"

Mikey nodded.

"Because I was **tired**, Mikey!" said Norm. "Why else do you think I fell asleep?"

"Well, obviously you were **tired**, Norm," said Mikey. "What I meant was **why?**"

"Why was I tired?"

"Yeah."

"Because I didn't go to bed till really late last night."

"Yes, but **why?**" persisted Mikey.

Gordon flipping Bennet, thought Norm. Was Mikey trying to set some kind of new world record for being incredibly annoying, or what? Because if he was, he was going about it the right way.

"If you must know, I was looking at bikes."

Mikey looked confused. "In a shop?"

"ON MY IPAD, YOU DOUGHNUT!"

"All right, all right," said Mikey. "There's no need to shout, Norm."

Straightaway Norm felt bad. It wasn't **Mikey's** fault he'd fallen asleep in class any more than it was Mikey's fault that he was just that little bit better at most things than Norm was. It was still frustrating though, having to explain. Like talking to one of his little brothers.

"Sorry, Mikey," said Norm.

"It's OK," said Mikey. "See anything you like?"

Norm thought for a moment. Had he seen anything he'd liked? Abso-flipping-lutely he had! But before he could reply, something smacked him between the eyes with such force, it felt like he'd been whacked round the head by an elephant's trunk. Not that Norm had ever actually **been** whacked round the head by an elephant's trunk before – but he imagined that's what it would feel like if he had been. It was all he could do to stay on his feet, let alone speak.

"WHAT A GOAL!" yelled a voice.

"You OK, Norm?" said Mikey.

"Uh? What?" said Norm. "What happened?"

"That was **amazing!**"

Norm turned round to see Connor Wright running up to him. "What was?"

Connor Wright laughed. "What do you mean what was? That was the most incredible header I've ever seen!"

Header? thought Norm.

"The keeper never stood a chance!"

Norm suddenly twigged. So **that's** what had hit him. A football! Not only that, but it appeared he'd somehow managed to score a goal!

"I thought you were kidding," said Connor Wright.

"What do you mean?" said Norm, who knew perfectly well what Connor Wright meant. What he'd said earlier about **choosing** not to play football was a load of garbage. He'd only said it to try and shut him up. But there was no way he was going to admit that **now**.

"When you said you were really good at football."

Norm shrugged. "Yeah, well, you know…"

Connor Wright eyed Norm suspiciously for a moment. "You did **mean** to, didn't you?"

"Mean to what?" said Norm.

"Head the ball?"

"Course I did," said Norm nonchalantly. "What? You think the ball just **hit** me or something?"

"No, I just…"

"What then?" said Norm.

"Nothing," said Connor Wright.

"Good," said Norm. "Now if you don't mind, my friend and I are **trying** to have a conversation."

Connor Wright showed no sign of moving.

"Go on," said Norm dismissively. "Run along and play now. There's a good boy."

Connor Wright turned to leave, but stopped again. "If you ever fancy a kick about...?"

"Yeah, yeah," said Norm. "I'll let you know."

Norm and Mikey watched as Connor Wright trotted off again.

"Can I ask you a question, Norm?"

Norm shrugged. "I dunno, Mikey. **Can** you?"

"What was all that about?"

"What was all **what** about?"

"You didn't **really** mean to head the ball, did you?"

"Are you **serious?**" said Norm.

Mikey nodded.

"Did I *mean* to head the ball?"

Mikey nodded again.

"Mikey?"

"Yeah?" said Mikey.

"There's more chance of me giving up flipping *pizza* than there is of me ever meaning to *head* a flipping football!"

"What?" said Mikey.

"Of *course* I didn't flipping mean to head it! It just flipping hit me!"

"That's what I thought," said Mikey.

"So why flipping ask then?" said Norm.

"Dunno," said Mikey. "I was just checking."

"Doughnut," said Norm as the bell rang signalling the end of lunch and the beginning of afternoon lessons.

CHAPTER 3

"Feeling all right, Norm?" said Mikey as he waited in the playground for his friend to catch up so that they could walk to the bike shed together.

"What?" said Norm. "Why shouldn't I be?"

"After your amazing 'header'?" said Mikey making speech marks in the air with his fingers.

"Shhhh!" hissed Norm, looking around anxiously. He didn't mind Mikey knowing that the goal he'd scored had been a complete and utter fluke, but he didn't want anyone **else** to know – especially Connor Wright. But there was no danger of being overheard by Connor Wright, or anybody else for that matter. School was over for another day. Kids were pouring out the main doors like a river of excitable ants, all talking and laughing at the tops of their voices.

"You must admit, it was quite funny," grinned Mikey.

"Funny?" said Norm.

Mikey nodded.

"You call being whacked on the head by a flipping football **funny?**"

Mikey stopped grinning and suddenly looked a bit sheepish. "Erm, well..."

"I tell you what's **funny**, Mikey," said Norm.

"What?" said Mikey.

Norm thought for a moment. He couldn't think of anything even remotely funny. It was **SO** flipping annoying.

"I'll get back to you."

"When?" said Mikey.

Norm sighed. "What do you mean, **when?** I don't know **when**, you doughnut!"

They walked on in stony silence for a few moments.

"Sorry, Norm," said Mikey eventually.

Norm shrugged. "It's all right."

"Really?"

Norm shrugged again. "S'pose."

Mikey looked instantly relieved. "Fancy going biking later?"

Norm couldn't help laughing. Did he fancy going biking later? What kind of stupid question was **that?** He **always** fancied going biking! He'd be out on his bike 24/7 if his mum and dad let him. Longer if possible.

"I'll take that as a yes, then?" said Mikey.

"What do **you** think, Mikey?"

"Great," said Mikey. "I'll call round for you once I've done my homework then."

Norm groaned.

"What's up?" said Mikey.

"That's just reminded me."

"What?"

"I've got a punishment exercise," said Norm.

"What for?" said Mikey. "Falling asleep in history?"

Norm nodded.

"What have you got to do, Norm?"

It was a good point actually, thought Norm. What **had** he got to do? It was so boring he'd almost fallen asleep again just writing it down!

"Something about kings and queens, I think. I'm not really sure."

"What about them?"

"I dunno, Mikey, all right?" said Norm irritably.

"All right," said Mikey. "I was just asking."

"Hang on a minute," said Norm. "When have I next got history?"

Mikey pulled a face. "I've no idea."

"I wasn't talking to you, Mikey," said Norm. "I was talking to myself."

Mikey looked concerned. "Are you *sure* you're all right, Norm?"

"YESSS!" said Norm, punching the air.

"What?" said Mikey, who by now was beginning to look genuinely worried.

"Tomorrow's Thursday, right?"

"Right," said Mikey.

"I don't have history tomorrow!" said Norm.

"So that means..."

"I **can** go biking tonight!" said Norm triumphantly.

"Great!" said Mikey.

Norm smiled. Despite the punishment exercise and being hit on the head by a football, today had just got a whole lot better. And it wasn't very often Norm could say **that**.

Norm was still smiling a few moments later when he and Mikey rounded a corner to see the bike shed with only one bike left in it. And it wasn't **his**.

"Now that really is funny, Mikey," said Norm.

"What is?" said Mikey, unlocking his bike.

"Where is it?"

"Where's what?" said Mikey innocently.

"Where's what?" mimicked Norm. "Er, *my* bike?"

Mikey shrugged. "Don't ask me."

"Come on, Mikey, stop mucking about. Where have you hidden it?"

"Why would I hide your bike?" said Mikey.

Norm began to get a horrible feeling in his stomach. Not the kind of feeling he got when he'd eaten too much pizza and he suddenly needed to find a toilet. A whole different *level* of horrible feeling.

"Seriously, Norm, I have no idea where your bike is."

Norm stared at Mikey. It was beginning to look like he was actually telling the truth. In fact in all the years they'd known each other, Norm couldn't recall Mikey ever trying to pull off any kind of stunt or practical joke. Why would he start **now?**

"So that means..."

Mikey nodded. "It's been stolen."

Norm had temporarily lost the power of speech. It didn't really matter though. Even if he **could** have spoken he wouldn't have known what to say. His bike was gone. Someone had taken it. **His** flipping bike! It made no difference that it was a **rubbish** bike. It was **his** rubbish bike! Not someone **else's** rubbish bike!

"I don't understand," said Mikey. "Someone must have known the combination.

Norm didn't reply.

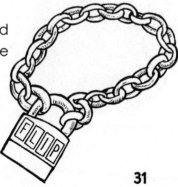

"You **did** lock it, didn't you, Norm?"

But Norm still didn't reply. He felt like he'd just run slap bang into a brick wall. Naked. And with the whole flipping school watching.

CHAPTER 4

"Who's that?" called Norm's dad anxiously from the kitchen, as soon as the front door slammed shut. Not that Norm actually noticed his dad sounding anxious. Then again Norm was so consumed with recent events, he wouldn't have noticed if the house had been on fire and his dad had been trying to put it out with a watering can.

"That you, Norman?"

"Yeah," said Norm, slouching into the kitchen like a slug with an attitude problem.

"Thank goodness for that," said Norm's dad, looking up from his newspaper.

"What?" said Norm.

Norm's dad grinned. "Well, I was supposed to be getting tea ready, wasn't I?"

Norm pulled a face. He couldn't care less what his dad was supposed to be doing at the **best** of times – let alone right now.

"Bit late, aren't you?" said Norm's dad, glancing up at the clock on the wall.

"Walked," mumbled Norm.

"You **walked?**" said Norm's dad as if Norm had just announced he'd taken up embroidery as a hobby.

"Had to," mumbled Norm.

"You **had** to?"

Norm nodded.

"You feeling OK, son?"

Norm said nothing.

"Norman?" said Norm's dad. "What's up? Has something happened?"

Norm nodded again.

"Well?" said Norm's dad. "Are you going to tell me **what's** happened, or am I going to have to guess?"

Norm sighed. This was no time for stupid guessing games. "Bike's been nicked."

Norm's dad put down his newspaper. "What did you say?"

"Bike's been nicked."

"Nicked?"

"Yeah."

"Stolen?" said Norm's dad.

"Yeah," said Norm. "Stolen."

"You're joking," said Norm's dad.

Joking? thought Norm. **Joking?** How long had his dad known him? Surely he knew by now that there were **some** things you just didn't joke about? Having his bike nicked was one of them.

"When?" said Norm's dad.

What? thought Norm. How was **he** supposed to know when his bike had been nicked?

"I dunno, Dad. I wasn't there at the time."

"Don't get smart with me, Norman," said Norm's dad, the vein on the side of his head beginning to throb – a sure-fire sign that he was starting to get stressed. Not that Norm noticed.

There was a sudden commotion outside. Norm heard the unmistakable sound of his brothers, squabbling and squawking like a pair of unruly parrots, together with the sound of his mum doing her best to keep them under control.

"Hello, boys," said Norm's dad as Brian and Dave exploded into the kitchen moments later, pursued by John the dog. "How was school?"

"Brilliant!" said Dave.

"All right," said Brian.

"Woof," said John.

"What's for tea, Dad?" said Dave.

"Yes, what is for tea, **Dad?**' said Norm's mum pointedly, appearing in the doorway.

"Erm..." began Norm's dad.

Norm's mum sighed. "You haven't just been sat there reading the paper all day, have you?"

"Erm, well," said Norm's dad. "The thing is..."

"The thing is," said Norm's mum, "you were supposed to have tea ready by the time we got back!"

"I know, but..."

"So why isn't it?"

"Well you see..."

"It's not like you've got anything **better** to do!" said Norm's mum.

Gordon flipping Bennet! thought Norm. Was it him, or was the whole flipping world going stark raving mad? Here he was – in the middle of a deeply traumatic personal crisis – and all everyone else was bothered about was flipping tea! OK so his mum and his brothers didn't actually **know**  about his bike yet. But that was beside the point.

"I'm starving!" said Dave.

"Woof," said John.

Brian laughed. "John said **he's** starving, as well!"

"No, he didn't!" snapped Norm.

"But..." began Brian.

"Shut it, you freak! He's a dog! He can't talk! End of!"

Everything suddenly went very quiet.

Norm's mum looked at Norm for a moment. "Something wrong, love?"

Norm and his dad exchanged a quick glance.

"What is it?" said Norm's mum. "What's happened?"

"You say, Dad," said Norm.

"What?" said Norm's mum.

"His bike's been stolen."

"Pardon?" said Norm's mum.

"Norman's bike," said Norm's dad. "It's been stolen."

"Oh, no," said Norm's mum. "When?"

"He doesn't know," said Norm's dad quickly, saving Norm the bother.

Norm's mum looked at Norm and did her best to smile sympathetically. "I'm sorry, love. That's really awful."

Norm didn't know what to say. What **could** he say? It wasn't just **awful**, it was pretty much the **worst** thing that had ever happened to him. And that **included** wetting the bed when he was eight. Which wouldn't have actually been so bad, except they'd been in IKEA at the time.

"Still," said Norm's mum, "it could be worse."

Uh? thought Norm. No it flipping **couldn't!** His flipping bike had been nicked!

"At least it's insured."

Norm's dad made a funny croaking noise.

"What's the matter?" said Norm's mum.

"Er, nothing," said Norm's dad getting up and heading for the fridge. "Better get cracking on that tea I suppose!"

"Alan?" said Norm's mum watching him go.

"Yes?" said Norm's dad breezily.

"I said at least Norman's bike is _**insured**_."

"Yes," laughed Norm's dad as he opened the fridge door. "Now let's see what we've got in here. Ooh, look. An aubergine!"

Not only did Norm have no idea what an aubergine actually was, he had a horrible feeling that he knew what was coming next.

"Please tell me you remembered to renew the insurance policy?" said Norm's mum.

"Erm..." said Norm's dad.

"You didn't, did you?"

"Does that mean..." began Norm.

"We can't claim for it and we won't get a penny," said his mum. "Exactly."

"Brilliant," said Norm.

Brian pulled a face. "What's brilliant about that?"

"Shut up, Brian, you freak!" spat Norm.

"So what *is* for tea, then?" said Dave.

CHAPTER 5

Tea, as it turned out, had consisted of spaghetti bolognaise. Not only was it Norm's dad's signature dish, it was one of the few things he could actually cook without it ending up looking like some kind of failed science experiment. Not that Norm had particularly cared what it was. He'd made his excuses and mooched off to his room at the earliest possible opportunity. The revelation that his bike wasn't insured had been the last flipping straw. Now all he wanted was to be left alone to watch videos on his iPad. At least for a *few* minutes.

Signature dish

There was a knock at the door.

"Norman?"

Gordon flipping Bennet! thought Norm. So much for being left alone.

Gordon Flipping Bennet

"Can I come in?" said Norm's mum without waiting for a reply and opening the door anyway.

"Hi, Mum."

"I thought you said you'd got homework to do?"

"Did I?" said Norm. "Don't remember that."

"Well, I do," said Norm's mum. "That was the only reason I let you leave the table before anybody else."

"How do you know I'm *not* doing homework?"

Norm's mum eyed Norm for a moment. "Well? **Are** you?"

Norm briefly considered telling a porky, but decided against it. "Er, no, Mum. I'm not."

"Well that's just not fair on your brothers!"

Norm pulled a face. "Why?"

"They're still tidying up down there."

"Good," mumbled Norm.

"Pardon?"

"Serves them flipping right."

"What for?"

Norm shrugged. "Being born."

"Mind if I come in for a minute?"

Actually, thought Norm, he did mind. As a matter of fact he minded very much. His mum coming into his room unannounced generally meant one of two things. Either she was about to nag him to tidy it up **or** she was about to ask him how he was **feeling** about something or other. Norm looked around. For once, his room was reasonably tidy.

"How are you feeling?" said Norm's mum sitting down at the end of the bed.

Norm sighed.

"Like that, is it, love?"

Like what? thought Norm. Like he'd just woken up from a nightmare about being chased down the street by an army of robot spiders – only to discover that it **wasn't** actually a nightmare after all and that he really was being chased down the road by a bunch of robot spiders? Because if so then yes – that was **exactly** what it was flipping like! Except worse.

"Do you want a hug?"

Of **course**, thought Norm. Because a flipping hug would make **everything** better, wouldn't it? Brilliant! Why hadn't he thought of that before?

"Well?" said Norm's mum.

"I'm nearly thirteen, Mum!" said Norm.

"Never too old for a hug, love," laughed Norm's mum. "Even your dad and I..."

"Please stop, Mum," said Norm, to whom the idea of his parents having **any** kind of physical contact was enough to make him lose his lunch.

Norm's mum looked at Norm for a moment. "Are you sure it was actually **stolen?**"

"What?" said Norm.

"Are you sure someone's not just…"

"What?"

"Well…borrowed it?"

Norm was confused. "***Borrowed*** it?"

Norm's mum nodded.

"Without asking?"

"Exactly."

"But…" began Norm.

"I'm just saying," said Norm's mum.

Uh? thought Norm. ***What*** was his mum saying? Because this was beginning to do his head in.

"There are two sides to every story, love."

Not to **this** one there flipping wasn't, thought Norm. His bike was gone. Someone who **shouldn't** have taken it **had** taken it. It didn't make any difference whether they'd flipping asked or not!

"Let's see if it turns up first, shall we?"

"What do you mean, **first**, Mum?"

"Before we call the police?"

Funnily enough, Norm hadn't actually thought of calling the police before. But now his mum came to mention it, that was an excellent idea.

"How long do you think we should wait, Mum?" said Norm. "Ten minutes?"

Norm's mum laughed. "A bit longer than that, love!"

"Half an hour?"

"I'll have a word tomorrow," said Norm's mum.

Tomorrow? thought Norm. His bike could be

halfway round the world by then! If it hadn't already been sold on eBay!

"Who with?"

"Your head teacher."

"What?"

"At parents' evening?" said Norm's mum.

Gordon flipping Bennet! thought Norm. Parents' evening? Tomorrow? Nobody told him anything!

"You hadn't forgotten about it, had you, love?"

"What?" said Norm. "No, course not, Mum. How could I possibly forget parents' evening? It's the highlight of my whole year."

"No need to be sarcastic, Norman."

Actually, thought Norm, his mum was right for once. On this occasion there really **was** no need to be sarcastic. It might make him **feel** better temporarily. But it wouldn't actually **change** anything.

"So **have** you?" said Norm's mum.

"Uh?" said Norm. "Have I **what**?"

"Got any homework?"

Norm sighed as he suddenly remembered the punishment exercise. "Not exactly, no."

Norm's mum looked puzzled. "Not exactly?"

"Erm, well it's not exactly homework, Mum."

"What is it then?" said Norm's mum.

"Just this…thing I've got to do."

"Well, don't let me keep you, love," said Norm's mum getting up and heading for the door.

"Pardon, Mum?"

"Better get on with it."

Right, thought Norm watching his mum disappear. Like *that* was going to happen.

CHAPTER 6

Left to his own devices at last, Norm stayed exactly where he was and continued doing exactly what he'd been doing before being so rudely interrupted by his mother. Why should he do his stupid punishment exercise, anyway? thought Norm. It wasn't like it was for tomorrow or anything. And besides, if he couldn't actually go biking himself, he might as well watch other people go biking instead. It was the next best thing.

At least that's what Norm had **_thought._** But it soon became apparent that it was just too painful watching other people riding bikes – especially watching other people riding bikes that Norm could only ever **dream** of owning. If only his mum had a **proper** job. If only his dad had a job full flipping stop! If only they hadn't had to move to this stupid little house because they were so flipping skint! If only his parents had stopped at one child! If only his dad had remembered to renew the insurance policy! If only Dave hadn't suddenly walked into his room without flipping knocking...

"Gordon flipping Bennet!" spat Norm.

"Language," said Dave.

"What do **you** want?"

"Charming," said Dave.

"Seriously," said Norm. "What do you want, Dave? Only I'm a bit busy right now."

Dave studied Norm for a moment.

"Really? You don't look very busy to me."

"Yeah, well I am, all right?"

"What are you doing?"

Norm sighed. "If you must know I'm looking at photos on Facebook."

"What of?" said Dave.

"Me and Mikey, biking."

Dave pulled a face. "Why don't you just go biking instead?"

Norm shot Dave
a look.

"Oh, sorry," said
Dave. "Forgot."

"Don't let me
keep you, Dave."

"Heard about the header by the way," said Dave showing no signs of going anywhere just yet.

"What?" said Norm.

"I heard about the header," said Dave. "You know? The goal you scored?"

Norm suddenly twigged what Dave was talking about.

"Oh, right. *That* header."

"*That* header?" said Dave. "You mean you've done more than one?"

Norm shrugged. "Might have done."

Dave pulled a face. "But you don't even *like* football!"

"I *hate* football," Norm corrected him.

"That's not nice, Norman."

"Uh?" said Norm. "What isn't?"

58

"To say you **hate** something," said Dave. "That's not nice."

"In that case," said Norm, "I strongly detest football."

"So..."

"What?"

"How come you were playing?"

"I wasn't," said Norm.

"But..."

"What?"

"You scored a goal!" said Dave.

Norm shrugged again. "I was just passing."

Dave looked very confused. "I thought it was a header?"

"What?" said Norm. "No. Look it's no big deal, Dave, all right?"

"Reece said it was amazing."

Norm looked at his little brother.

"Who's Reece?"

"Reece Wright?"

"Right," said Norm. "And how does *he* know?"

"His brother told him," said Dave.

"Who's his brother?"

"Connor Wright?"

"Oh, right," said Norm. "I didn't even know he *had* a brother."

Dave nodded. "He's my *seventh* best friend."

It was Norm's turn to be confused now. "Who is? Connor?"

"No, Reece."

"You've got seven best friends?"

"What?" laughed Dave. "No, I mean he's not my **best** friend. He's my **seventh** best friend!"

"You've got like, a league table of best friends?" said Norm.

Dave pulled a face. "Hasn't everyone?"

"Er, **no!**" said Norm.

"Weird," said Dave.

Norm couldn't help smiling. Although it was fair to say that **both** his brothers bugged the heck out of him, it was **also** fair to say that **Dave** tended to bug the heck out of him  ever so slightly **less** and ever so slightly less **often** than Brian did. On occasions, they'd even been known to actually get **on** with each other for short periods. Usually **very** short periods.

"So what **do** you want, Dave?"

"What?" said Dave.

"You didn't just come here to tell me that you'd heard about the header."

"Might've done," said Dave.

"Yeah, but you didn't, Dave, did you?"

Dave sighed. "Mum sent me to check what you were doing."

"Seriously?"

Dave nodded.

"Mum sent you to **spy** on me?"

Dave nodded again.

"Unbelievable," said Norm. "Unbe-flipping-lievable."

"Language," said Dave.

"Shut up, Dave, you little freak."

"I'm telling."

"What?"

"I'm telling Mum."

"Telling her what?" said Norm. "That I told you to shut up, or that I wasn't doing my punishment exercise?"

Norm realised straightaway what he'd done. The question was, had **Dave** realised too?

"You've got a punishment exercise?"

Flip, thought Norm. He'd realised.

"Don't say anything, Dave," said Norm. "Please?"

Dave narrowed his eyes as he weighed up his options.

"What's it worth?"

Norm shrugged. "Dunno. What do you reckon?"

Dave thought for a moment before slowly smiling from ear to ear.

"Fancy a kick about in the garden?"

"A kick about?"

"Yeah," said Dave.

"With a ball, you mean?"

Dave laughed. "What else?"

What else? thought Norm. He could think of several things he'd like to kick right now – including himself! What a flipping doughnut – accidentally letting slip about the punishment exercise.

"Come on then," said Norm putting his iPad down and getting up off his bed. "Let's get it over with."

"Yeah!" squeaked Dave with excitement. "Bagsy me go in goal!"

"Whatever," said Norm following his little brother out the door.

CHAPTER 7

It didn't take Norm very long to remember **why** he 'strongly detested' football quite so much. Football, in Norm's opinion, was completely pointless. A load of blokes running around a field like headless chickens, falling over whenever anyone came anywhere near them? What was all **that** about? At least with mountain biking there was a very definite beginning and an end. It was all about who could get from A to B the quickest.

Preferably **without** getting up close and personal with a rock or wrapping yourself round a tree in the process. Never mind the fact that the closest thing to a mountain where Norm lived was the woods behind the shopping precinct. That wasn't the point. The point **was** that football was completely pointless. So how come it was so popular? Norm just didn't get it at all.

"Come on, Norman!" said Dave.

"What?" said Norm.

"Take another shot!"

"Another?" said Norm. "Do I **have** to?"

Dave grinned. "Yes you **do** have to, actually! We made a deal, remember?"

Norm sighed. "How much longer?"

"Till you actually score a goal!"

Gordon flipping Bennet! thought Norm. Till he scored a **goal?** He must have had at least **ten** shots already. And Dave **still** hadn't had to make a single save! He'd grow a flipping beard first at this rate!

"Come on!" said Dave.

"All right, all right," said Norm irritably. "What's the hurry?"

"It's going to be dark soon," said Dave. "**That's** the hurry!"

"Why don't I go in goal and you take shots, Dave?"

"It's fine," said Dave. "I *like* being in goal."

"Whatever," said Norm taking a couple of steps back and staring intently at the ball. If he could just concentrate for a moment and give it his best shot – *literally* give it his *best* shot – he could be back in his room and watching biking videos in next to no time.

"Mum says she's going to buy me some proper goalie gloves," said Dave.

Norm looked slowly up from the ball. "What did you just say?"

"Mum says she's going to buy me some goalie gloves," said Dave. "And a proper goalie shirt as well."

"You mean for your *birthday?*" said Norm.

"Nah," said Dave.

"Christmas?" said Norm.

"Nah," said Dave.

"What for then?"

"Dunno," said Dave.

"You mean..."

"What?"

"She's just going to **buy** you them?"

"Yeah," said Dave.

"For no reason whatso-flipping-ever?"

"Lang..." began Dave.

"Don't even flipping **think** about it, Dave," said Norm.

"But..."

"What?" said Norm.

"What's the matter, Norman?"

"What's the matter?" Norm repeated.

"I asked first," said Dave.

"I'll tell you what the flipping *matter* is Dave!" said Norm. "I've just had my bike nicked!"

"Yeah, I know," said Dave. "But that's not *my* fault."

"Yeah well it's not *my* flipping fault either, Dave!" said Norm getting more and more wound up.

"So it was locked up then?"

"Flipping wish *you* were," muttered Norm.

"What was that?" said Dave.

"Nothing," said Norm.

"I'm sorry."

"What about?" said Norm.

"Your bike."

Norm snorted. "**You're** sorry? How do you think **I** flipping feel?"

Dave thought for a moment. "I can't imagine."

"It wasn't **insured**, Dave."

"Yeah, I know."

"So that means I'm not going to get any flipping money for it and Mum says they can't afford to buy me another one."

"Yeah, I know."

"And then you turn round and say you're getting goalie gloves and a flipping shirt bought for you just like that?"

Dave looked confused. "I didn't turn **round** and say it."

"Unbe-flipping-lievable," said Norm heading back towards the house.

Unbe-flipping-lievable

"Hey, what are you doing?" said Dave.

"What does it look like I'm doing?" said Norm. "I'm going in."

"But..."

"What?" snapped Norm.

"You haven't scored yet!"

"Yeah? So?" said Norm.

"I'll tell Mum!" said Dave.

"Tell Mum what?" said Norm's mum appearing in the doorway as if by magic.

Norm and Dave exchanged a quick glance.

"Nothing," said Dave.

"Sure?" said Norm's mum.

Dave nodded. "Sure, Mum."

"What are you doing out here anyway, Norman?" said Norm's mum. "I thought you had something to do."

Norm thought for a moment. As a matter of fact he **did** have something to do. And he was going to do it right now. Something that might just make him feel just a **teensy** bit better. At least for a few seconds.

"AAAAAAAAAAAAAGH!" screamed Norm at the top of his voice, before suddenly charging towards the ball and kicking it as hard as he could.

AAAAAAAAAGH!!!!

"WHAT A GOAL!" squealed Dave, picking himself up off the ground.

Uh? What? thought Norm. How did **that** happen? He'd meant to boot the ball over the fence and as far away as possible! He hadn't actually **meant** to score at all!

"That was awesome, Norman!" said Dave.

Norm tried to shrug modestly. "Yeah, well, you know."

"Seriously!" said Dave. "I doubt I would've saved it even **with** my new goalie gloves on!"

Gordon flipping Bennet! thought Norm. So much for feeling **better!** Never mind a **few** seconds. That was barely even **two** seconds!

"Take another."

"Another what?" said Norm.

"Another shot," said Dave. "Just to prove it wasn't a fluke."

"Not now, Dave," said Norm's mum. "It's way past your bed time."

"Ah, Muuuum!" wailed Dave. "That's not fair!"

"Welcome to my world," muttered Norm, already halfway back to the house.

CHAPTER 8

One direct consequence of Norm being unexpectedly bikeless was having to get a lift to school from his dad the following day. This – as far as Norm was concerned – was **almost** as bad as having his bike nicked in the **first** place. Because, as far as **Norm** was concerned, having one or more of your parents show up at school was the single most embarrassing thing that could ever happen to you – with the possible exception of suddenly finding yourself naked in a supermarket. But that didn't actually

count because it turned out to be just a dream. **This,** on the other hand, was most definitely happening.

JABBER
JABBER
JABBER

What made things even **worse** for Norm was having to **share** the lift with his little brothers. Having Brian and Dave sitting in the back of the car jabbering continuous nonsense the entire journey was like the icing on a particularly lousy cake.

"Shut up, you two!" snapped Norm when he couldn't stand it any longer. "You're driving me round the flipping bend!"

"Actually, Norman," said Brian, "I think you'll find it's **Dad** who's driving you round the bend."

"Good one, Brian!" giggled Dave.

"Yeah," said Norm. "Hilarious, Brian. You should be a comedian."

"Do you think so?" said Brian.

"I think he was being sarcastic," said Dave.

"Oh," said Brian.

"I thought it was quite funny actually," said Norm's dad.

"Thanks, Dad," said Brian.

"Don't mention it," said Norm's dad.

Gordon flipping Bennet, thought Norm. How much more of this was he expected to take? If only he could dive through the window and make his escape when they stopped at the next set of lights like he was in some kind of action movie or computer game or

something. But this was **real** life, thought Norm. And real life wasn't nearly as exciting. Real life was basically rubbish.

Norm sighed. He only had himself to blame for being stuck in the car. If he'd got out of bed as soon as his alarm had gone off instead of looking at bikes on his iPad again he might have actually had enough time to **walk** to school. Then again, if his mum or dad had actually **checked** that he'd got out of bed as soon as his alarm had gone off, he probably wouldn't have been late. So thinking about it, thought Norm, thinking about it, it wasn't actually his fault at all that he was stuck in the flipping car with his jabbering brothers. It was his mum and dad's.

"All set, Norman?" said Norm's dad.

"Uh? What?" said Norm.

"I said are you all set?"

"For what?" said Norm.

"For **school!**" said Norm's dad.

"Oh, right," said Norm. "Erm, not really, no."

"What have you got, first thing?"

Norm tried to think. It was a good question. What **had** he got first thing?

"Er, French, I **think.**"

"French, eh?" said Norm's dad. "Très bon!"

"What?" said Norm.

"It means 'very good'," piped up Brian from the back.

"What's French for 'shut your mouth, you little freak'?" muttered Norm.

"We'll have less of that, thank you," said Norm's dad.

"Yeah, Norman," said Brian.

"Yeah, Norman," said Dave.

Norm took a deep breath and exhaled again slowly. Outside, more and more kids were converging from side streets and heading towards school.

"By the way, there's no need to drop me right outside, Dad," said Norm.

"Pardon?" said Norm's dad.

"Here's just fine, thanks," said Norm.

"But we're nowhere near your school yet, Norman."

"Exactly," said Norm.

"You're not embarrassed, are you?" laughed Norm's dad.

"What?" said Norm. "Course not, Dad."

"So why do you want me to drop you here, then?"

"Yeah, Norman," said Brian.

"Yeah, Norman," said Dave.

"I'll drop you outside," said Norm's dad. "I've got to go that way, anyway, to get to the boys' school."

Great, thought Norm, slumping lower in his seat, in

the hope that no one looking into the car would be able to recognise him.

"I might even start singing," said Norm's dad.

Norm was utterly horrified. "WHAT?"

"What do you think, boys?" said Norm's dad glancing in the rear-view mirror. "Should I start singing?"

"YEAH!" said Brian and Dave together. "SING! SING! SING!"

Don't, don't, don't, thought Norm.

"Any requests?" said Norm's dad.

"Yeah, I've got one," said Norm.

"What's that, son?"

"Can you let me out now, please?"

Norm's dad laughed.

"I'm not joking, Dad," said Norm, starting to sound more and more desperate. "**_Please_** let me out!"

"Why? Don't you think I've got a good voice, or something?"

Norm pulled a face. "Are you serious, Dad? You sound like a goose with toothache!"

"That's stupid," chirped Brian.

"What is?" said Norm.

"Geese don't **_have_** teeth."

Norm turned round and glared at Brian. "Neither will you if you're not careful, you little freak."

"I heard that," said Norm's dad. "Now pack it in!"

"Yeah, Norman," said Brian.

"Yeah, Norman," said Dave.

"**All** of you," said Norm's dad, the vein on the side of his head beginning to throb.

"Sorry, Dad," said Brian.

"Yeah sorry, Dad," said Dave.

Flipping creeps, thought Norm as they approached the school gates and began to slow down.

"OOOH YEAH, BABY!" sang Norm's dad, whilst simultaneously opening all the windows for maximum effect. "I LOVE YOU SOOOOOOOO!"

This was it then, thought Norm. The day when he finally lost the last shreds of what little street cred he'd had in the first flipping place. The day he officially became a laughing stock in front of the whole flipping school. The day that would surely go down in history as by far the most **humiliating** day of his life.

"Bye then, Norman," said Norm's dad pulling up by the kerb.

"Bye," mumbled Norm opening the door and getting out.

"Take care."

Yeah, thought Norm. And what a stupid flipping thing **that** was to say. Take care. As if he **wouldn't** have done if his dad hadn't said anything.

"MIND OUT, NORM!" yelled Mikey, skidding on his bike and only just avoiding hitting his best friend.

"Gordon flipping Bennet, Mikey!" said Norm. "Watch where you're going, you doughnut!"

"Me?" said Mikey. "Watch where I'm going? How about you watch where **you're** going, Norm?"

"Hi, Mikey," said Norm's dad.

"Yeah! Bikey Mikey!" squeaked Brian and Dave from the back of the car.

"Well," said Norm's dad. "Can't stop."

"Thank goodness for that," muttered Norm under his breath.

"What was that, Norman?"

"Nothing, Dad," said Norm, closing the car door.

"Have a good day, boys!" yelled Norm's dad driving off.

"We will," said Mikey.

"Speak for yourself," said Norm.

Mikey pulled a face. "What's up, Norm?"

"What's up?" said Norm, heading into school. "What's flipping **not?**"

CHAPTER 9

"How was your morning, Norm?" said Mikey when the pair met up that lunchtime and began walking round the school grounds together as per usual.

What kind of stupid question was *that?* wondered Norm. How was his morning? Pretty much like *most* flipping mornings at school!

"Have a wild guess, Mikey."

"Rubbish?" said Mikey.

"Correct," said Norm.

"Why's that, then?"

"Just flipping was, all right?"

"Fair enough."

They walked on for a few more seconds.

"Mine was fine, by the way, thanks for asking," said Mikey.

Norm pulled a face. "I **didn't** ask."

"I know," said Mikey pointedly. "That's what I meant."

They walked on for a few more seconds before Mikey broke the silence once again.

"No news then?"

"What about?"

"You know?" said Mikey.

"No, I **don't** know actually, Mikey," said Norm. "What?"

Mikey hesitated slightly, as if he was unsure whether to go on or not.

"Your bike?"

"Oh, right," said Norm. "Nah."

"That's a shame."

Norm turned and looked at Mikey. Sometimes he genuinely wondered how they'd managed to remain friends for quite as long as they had. **This** was one of those sometimes.

"A shame?"

Mikey nodded.

"A *shame?*"

"Well, you know..." began Mikey.

"It's more than a *shame*, Mikey," said Norm. "It's an abso-flipping-lute disaster!"

Mikey briefly thought about saying something, but didn't. He knew better than to argue with Norm when Norm was in a mood like this.

"You reported it to the police yet?"

"Not yet," said Norm. "Mum says she's going to have a word at parents' evening tonight."

"Cool," said Mikey.

"No, Mikey, not cool," said Norm. "Not cool at all."

"Hey, Norman," said a voice.

Norm turned around to see Connor Wright walking towards them.

"How's it going?"

"Not good," said Mikey before Norm had a chance to answer for himself. "He's had his bike stolen."

"I *can* actually speak thanks, Mikey," said Norm.

"Yeah, I heard about that," said Connor Wright.

"What?" said Norm. "You heard that I can speak?"

"No," said Connor Wright. "I heard your bike had been nicked."

"Oh right," said Norm. "Who from?"

"My brother," said Connor Wright.

Mikey turned to Norm. "Your bike's been nicked from Connor's brother?"

"What?" said Norm. "No, you doughnut! His brother **told** him that my bike's been nicked!"

"Oh," said Mikey.

"His brother knows Dave."

"Right," said Mikey. "I see."

"Yeah, funny that, isn't it?" said Connor Wright.

"Hilarious," said Norm, beginning to wonder exactly why Connor Wright was still there. Come to think of it, why had he come over in the first place? What was he doing being all palsy-walsy all of a sudden?

"Yeah, so anyway..." began Connor Wright.

"What?" said Norm.

"I was wondering what you were doing on Saturday?"

Uh? thought Norm. Well, **this** was a bit unexpected. Well actually it was more than a **bit** unexpected. It was a complete whatsit. A thingy from the thing. A bolt from the blue. That was what it was, thought Norm. A bolt from the blue. Whatever one of **those** was. What was he doing on **Saturday?** He had no idea. All he knew was that he had no intention of spending any of it with Connor flipping Wright if he could possibly help it.

"Norman?"

"Sorry, what?" said Norm.

"I said I was wondering what you're doing on Saturday?"

"Saturday?"

Connor Wright nodded. "The day after tomorrow?"

"I know when Saturday is," said Norm.

Mikey laughed.

"Well?" said Connor Wright.

"Biking," said Norm.

Connor Wright frowned. "So you've got more than one bike, then?"

"What?"

"Well if your bike's been stolen..."

"Oh right, yeah, I forgot about that," said Norm.

"You forgot your bike was stolen?" said Connor Wright doubtfully. "We were just talking about it, like, two seconds ago or something."

Norm, by now, was starting to get pretty irritated.

Was Connor Wright going to hurry up and say what was on his mind, or what? Because if not, he'd.... he'd....he'd. Well he'd do **something**. He just couldn't think what.

"Anyway," said Connor Wright, "we're a man short."

"What?"

"We're a man short. For the match."

Norm literally had no idea what Connor Wright was talking about. What did he **mean,** they were a **man short?** Did you have to be a certain height to play or something?

"We don't have enough **players**."

"Oh, right," said Norm. "I see."

Connor Wright frowned. "What did you **_think_** I meant?"

"Nothing. I was just..."

"So do you wanna play?"

Norm pulled a face. Had Connor Wright really just said what he **_thought_** he'd just said? Surely not.

"What?" said Norm.

"Fancy a game?"

Norm smiled. "Do I fancy a game of **_football?_**"

Connor Wright nodded. "I told Mr Perry about the goal. He says you don't even need a trial and that you can play if you want."

"Seriously?"

Connor Wright nodded again. "Seriously."

"Yeah right," laughed Norm.

"Brilliant," said Connor Wright. "Sorted."

Norm's face dropped like a stone. "What? No, I meant yeah right as in, you know...**_yeah right?_**"

"You mean..."

"Yeah," said Norm. "I was being sarcastic."

"So that's a no, then?"

"Yes it's a no," said Norm.

"Why?" said Connor Wright.

"Why?" said Norm.

"Yeah," said Connor Wright.

Norm sighed. "Because I'd sooner...sooner... sooner..."

Mikey thought for a moment. "Snog a halibut?"

"Exactly," said Norm. "I'd sooner snog a halibut than play football on Saturday. Thank you, Mikey."

"You're welcome," said Mikey.

"But..." began Connor Wright.

"What?" said Norm.

"It was an **amazing** goal!"

"Yeah, so?" said Norm.

"So you might actually score **another** one on Saturday! And we're a man short!"

Gordon flipping Bennet! thought Norm. Which part of **no** did Connor Wright not understand? It was like trying to have a conversation with a flipping chair. Except at least you could **sit** on a chair afterwards.

BLAH BLAH BLAH

"Come on, Norman."

"Nah," said Norm.

"You **know** you want to."

"I **know** I flipping don't," said Norm.

"That's a pity."

"No it flipping isn't," said Norm beginning to walk away. "Come on, Mikey."

"What? Oh, right," said Mikey following.

"Well, if you change your mind..." called Connor Wright, watching them go.

Norm couldn't help chuckling quietly to himself. Change his mind? There was more chance of changing **parents** than there was of him ever changing his **mind!** And **that** was never going to happen. Worst flipping luck.

"Mikey?" said Norm.

"Yeah?"

"What's a halibut?"

"A kind of fish," laughed Mikey.

Norm pulled a face. "Really?"

"Yeah," said Mikey. "Still sooner snog one than play football on Saturday?"

"Abso-flipping-lutely!" said Norm.

CHAPTER 10

Norm was in no great rush to get home after school that day. There was no point. It wasn't as if he was going to be able to go biking. All he could do was drool over yet *more* impossibly cool looking bikes – none of which he stood even the slightest chance of ever actually *owning*, thanks to his stingy mum and dad.

Plodding slowly along the pavement, it suddenly occurred to Norm to go via the allotments to see if Grandpa was there. A dose of Grandpa was *exactly* what Norm needed right now. Grandpa wouldn't keep banging on about boring homework and stuff, thought Norm. At least he flipping *hoped* not anyway. Grandpa wasn't like most old people. He didn't constantly preach and turn everything into a flipping lecture and talk down to you as if you were only ten minutes old and knew next to nothing. Not that he tried to be all cool and trendy and young either, thank goodness, thought Norm. Because that would be **seriously** embarrassing.

"Hello, hello," said Grandpa when he saw Norm trudging forlornly up the path.

"Hi, Grandpa," said Norm.

"As the man said to the horse – why the long face?"

"What?" said Norm.

"You look like someone just peed in your porridge."

Norm was getting confused. He didn't even **like** porridge. And what was that about a horse? Perhaps coming to the allotments hadn't been **such** a good idea after all.

"What's up?"

"Oh, right," said Norm finally twigging what Grandpa meant. "Nothing much."

Grandpa raised his cloud-like eyebrows. "Nothing much?"

Norm shrugged.

"Come on, Norman. I can tell **something's** wrong. Spit it out."

"I've had my bike nicked."

"What?" said Grandpa.

"I've had my bike nicked."

Grandpa looked at Norm for a moment. "Stolen?"

Norm nodded.

"Whoa," said Grandpa. "Bummer."

"That's one way of putting it," said Norm.

"When?"

"Yesterday."

"Where was it?"

"At school," said Norm.

"Hmmm," said Grandpa. "So that's why you walked here. I thought it was a bit odd."

Norm didn't say anything. There was nothing **to** say. It was – as Grandpa had already pointed out – a bummer.

"Any ideas?" said Grandpa.

Norm pulled a face. "Ideas?"

"Who might have done it?"

"Oh, right," said Norm. "Nah."

"Hmmm," said Grandpa again, frowning until his

eyebrows met in the middle to form one enormous cloud. "It **was** insured, right?"

Norm sighed and shook his head.

"It wasn't insured?" said Grandpa in disbelief.

"Dad forgot to renew the whatsit," said Norm.

"The policy?"

Norm nodded.

"Oh for goodness sake," said Grandpa. "I told your mum not to marry him. But she wouldn't listen."

This was another thing that Norm loved about Grandpa. Grandpa was never afraid to speak his mind. Stuff that some people might only **think** – Grandpa actually **said**. It was like he was some kind of straight-talking superhero.

"I can see I'm going to have to have a word."

"Who with?" said Norm.

"Your dad," said Grandpa. "Honestly, of all the stupid things. It's not like he's got anything *else* to do."

True, thought Norm. What exactly *did* his dad do all day apart from going round the house switching things off to save electricity? He certainly didn't seem to be doing much about getting another flipping job that was for sure. If his dad hadn't gone and got himself sacked, it wouldn't have actually *mattered* if he'd remembered to renew the insurance policy or not. He could have just gone out and bought Norm a new bike! Some people were just so flipping inconsiderate!

"Which reminds me," said Grandpa.

"What, Grandpa?"

"I'm babysitting tonight."

"Who for?"

"Who for?" said Grandpa.

"Yeah," said Norm.

"You, you great wally!"

"Me?" said Norm.

"Isn't there a parents' evening, or something?" said Grandpa.

"Oh, right, yeah," said Norm, suddenly remembering. "But I don't need babysitting."

"Maybe **you** don't," said Grandpa. "But your brothers certainly do."

Good point, thought Norm. He didn't mind being left **alone** in his own house. But being left with his little **brothers?** He'd sooner be left with a flock of flipping hyenas. Or whatever the right word for more than one hyena was.

"In fact," said Grandpa looking at his watch, "I'd better get cracking. And you'd better get going, Norman."

"Yeah, 'spose so," said Norm, turning round and trudging back the way he'd come.

"See you soon," said Grandpa.

"See you soon, Grandpa," said Norm.

"Oh and Norman?"

"Yeah?"

"Sorry about your bike."

"Tell me about it," muttered Norm heading down the path.

CHAPTER 11

Norm had scarcely finished scoffing down his supermarket own-brand fish fingers, supermarket own-brand baked beans and supermarket own-brand oven chips before the doorbell rang.

"YEEEEAH! GRANDPAAAAAAA!" yelled Brian and Dave, charging headlong towards the hall, each desperately trying to get to the door before the other.

Norm watched them go. With any luck Grandpa would keep them occupied until his parents got back – leaving him in peace to do whatever he wanted to do for an hour or so. He wasn't actually sure what that would be yet. All he knew was that it wouldn't be involving his smelly little brothers.

"Won't be long, love," said Norm's mum getting up from the table.

"Be as long as you want, Mum."

Norm's mum smiled. "Charming."

"I just meant…"

"It's OK, love," she laughed. "Anything we should know, by the way?"

"What?" said Norm.

"Before the parents' evening?"

Norm laughed nervously. "Oh, right, yeah. Er, no, don't think so."

Norm's mum eyeballed him for a second. "You don't **think** so?"

"Yeah," said Norm. "I mean no. I mean..."

"What's the matter?"

"Nothing, Mum."

"Sure?"

Norm nodded. "Sure, Mum."

A car horn tooted.

"Better not keep Dad waiting, eh?" said Norm.

"You trying to get rid of me, love?"

"What?" said Norm. "No, course not, Mum!"

"Hmmm," said Norm's mum heading out the door. "See you later then."

"Missing you already," muttered Norm under his breath.

"I **heard** that!" called Norm's mum from the hall.

Gordon flipping Bennet! thought Norm. Another couple of seconds of cross-examination and he might well have cracked and told his mum about the punishment exercise which he **still** hadn't flipping done. The question was – would she and his dad find out about it at parents' evening? Because if they **did** there were **bound** to be percussions – or whatever the word was. Norm thought for a moment. Repercussions. That was it. There were bound to be **repercussions**. There always flipping were whenever **he** did something wrong. **He** only had to forget to flush the flipping toilet and he'd be banned from the Xbox for a flipping month or something! Not like his brothers. **They** could blow the flipping house up and his mum and dad wouldn't bat a flipping eyelid! It was so unfair.

Norm sighed. There was nothing much he could do about it now. It was in the laptop of the gods – or whatever the expression was. Whatever. It was out of his hands, basically. He just had to hope that Miss Rogers somehow forgot to mention to his mum and dad about him falling asleep in class the previous morning. If she didn't, there was every chance he'd be grounded till he was thirty.

"No news, then?" said Grandpa walking into the kitchen.

News? thought Norm. What about? The search for life on Mars? The Prime Minister's secret fondness for carpets? The discovery of an entirely new species of pizza?

Prime Minister

"About your bike?"

"What?" said Norm. "No, but I only saw you, like, five minutes ago or something, Grandpa."

"More like **_thirty_**-five," said Grandpa.

"Whatever," said Norm. "It wasn't very long ago."

Grandpa shrugged. "Well, you never know. It might have turned up."

Norm sighed . As a matter of fact he **_did_** know. Someone had taken his bike. He didn't know **_who'd_** taken it – or where they'd taken it to. But it was gone. And as far as Norm knew it was gone for-flipping-ever.

"Come on, Grandpa!" said Brian and Dave, suddenly bursting into the kitchen and attempting to drag and push Grandpa towards the back door.

"Whoa! Steady Eddy!" protested Grandpa. "I've only just got here!"

"WOOF!" went John, bounding in and jumping up at Grandpa, wagging his tail furiously.

"Look, Grandpa!" said Brian. "John wants you to play too!"

Grandpa sighed loudly.

"You promised, Grandpa!" wailed Dave.

"Did I?" said Grandpa. "I can't remember. I'm very old, you know."

"You're not old, Grandpa!" giggled Brian. "You're only, like, ninety-five or something!"

"Right, that's it," said Grandpa plonking himself down at the table, opposite Norm. "I'm having a kip first."

"But..." began Dave.

"But nothing," said Grandpa. "I'm having a kip."

"But..." began Brian.

"Do you actually want me to play, or not, boys?" said Grandpa.

"YEAH!" yelled Brian and Dave together.

"In that case, I'll be out in a minute," said Grandpa.

"Promise, Grandpa?" said Dave.

"Promise," said Grandpa. "Now clear off. Both of you."

Brian and Dave did as they were told and promptly cleared off.

"WOOF!" went John following them out into the garden.

"What are they like?" said Grandpa shaking his head.

"How long have you got?" muttered Norm darkly.

Grandpa's eyes crinkled ever so slightly in the

corners. It was the closest he ever came to smiling.

"Play what, by the way?"

"Football," said Grandpa.

Norm pulled a face. "Football?"

Grandpa nodded.

"I didn't know you played football, Grandpa."

"Ah, that's because I'm an international man of mystery," said Grandpa mysteriously.

"Uh?" said Norm. "You mean like a spy, or something?"

"Exactly."

"What?"

"You've got me," said Grandpa. "I'm actually a spy. My shed in the allotments is really the headquarters of a secret international organisation. Sorry I've never told you before, Norman. But there was never a good time."

Norm and Grandpa looked at each other for a couple of seconds before Grandpa's eyes eventually crinkled in the corners again.

"Yeah, yeah, very funny, Grandpa," said Norm. "Seriously though. Since when did you play football?"

"Since I was a kid."

"Whoa," said Norm.

"What?" said Grandpa.

"I didn't know football was even **_invented_** when **_you_** were a kid."

"Don't **_you_** start," said Grandpa.

"Sorry, Grandpa," grinned Norm. "I just never knew, that's all."

"I've told you before, Norman. There's a lot you don't know about me."

"GRANDPAAAAAAAAA!" bellowed Brian and Dave from the garden.

"Oh well," said Grandpa getting to his feet and heading for the back door. "No rest for the wicked."

"What else, Grandpa?"

"Pardon?"

"What *else* don't I know about you?"

"Ah, now that would be telling, wouldn't it?" said Grandpa, disappearing outside.

CHAPTER 12

It wasn't easy trying to watch videos on his iPad what with all the racket going on outside, but Norm was doing his best. Even **with** his headphones on though – and even though he was upstairs in his bedroom – he could **still** hear his brothers shrieking hysterically and John yapping away dementedly as if he'd never been in the garden before.

Gordon flipping Bennet! thought Norm. Did Brian and Dave really **have** to be quite so loud **all** the time? It was like they were in some kind of never-ending competition to see who could be heard the furthest away or something. Norm knew from experience that telling them to be quiet would have no effect whatso-flipping-ever. In fact, in Norm's experience, telling his brothers to be quiet usually had completely the **opposite** effect! They just got even louder. If only they had a volume control, thought Norm. Yeah. And an on/off button, too. That would be even *more* useful.

Then, all of a sudden, two things happened. Firstly something popped up on Norm's iPad, telling him that he'd received a message on Facebook. And secondly - something actually *did* pop in the garden. After that, everything went very quiet. About flipping time too, thought Norm, opening up the message.

Norm stared at the screen. Connor Wright? What did *he* want? They weren't even friends in *real* life – let alone on flipping Facebook! And what did he *mean*, "All right?" Honestly, thought Norm. What a flipping nerve. He'd a good mind to...to...to...

Norm sighed. He couldn't think *what* he had a good mind to do. And in any case another message had just appeared.

"Sorry I called you a geek. Didn't mean to."

Should flipping hope not too, thought Norm. There was nothing geeky about mountain biking. Mountain biking required skill, stamina and, above all else, **nerves of steel**. Actually, thought Norm, that wasn't quite right. What mountain biking required above all else was something he didn't actually **have** at the moment. A flipping bike! But there was no time to dwell on that either because Connor Wright had just sent **another** message.

"If you change your mind we're still a man short for Saturday."

"No!" said Norm out loud. "No, no, no, no, nooooo!"

"I'll take that as a no, then?" said Grandpa appearing in Norm's doorway.

"Oh hi, Grandpa," said Norm looking up.

"Mind if I come in?"

"Would it make any difference if I said yes, I did?" said Norm.

Grandpa thought for a moment. "Probably not, no."

"In that case, you'd better come in," said Norm.

"Thanks," said Grandpa walking into Norm's room and plonking himself down on the end of his bed.

"What was that popping sound, Grandpa?"

"Not guilty," said Grandpa.

"No, I meant out in the garden just now?"

"Oh, that?" said Grandpa. "Brian just exploded."

"What?"

"I'm kidding," said Grandpa. "It was the ball."

"The ball?" said Norm.

Grandpa nodded. "John burst it."

Norm laughed. "Really?"

"Bit it," said Grandpa.

"That's funny," said Norm.

"Your brothers didn't think so."

"Even better then."

"Now, now, Norman," said Grandpa. "'No **what**', by the way?"

"What?" said Norm. "Oh, right. It's just …"

"What?" said Grandpa. "I'm on the edge of my seat here. Well – the edge of your bed, anyway."

"This kid…"

"What kid?"

"Connor Wright," said Norm.

"What about him?" said Grandpa.

"He wants me to play football."

Grandpa waited for Norm to go on. But he didn't.

"And…?"

"That's it," said Norm.

"That's it?" said Grandpa.

Norm nodded.

"This Connor Wright wants you to play football? And you don't want to?"

"Correct," said Norm.

"Hmmm," said Grandpa. "Well I suppose that **is** a bit unreasonable of him."

Norm knew that Grandpa was being sarcastic. Which was annoying for a start, thought Norm. Because it was OK for **him** to be sarcastic. But not anybody else.

"You don't understand, Grandpa."

"Enlighten me."

"Uh? What?"

"Explain to me **why** I don't understand you."

"Oh, right," said Norm. "Well it's not just a kick about."

"What is it, then?" said Grandpa.

"It's a proper match."

"I see. And what's so terrible about playing a proper match of football, Norman?"

"I just don't **want** to," said Norm. "I'd sooner snog a halibut."

"A **halibut?**" said Grandpa.

"Yeah," said Norm. "Or any other kind of fish for that matter."

"Why?" said Grandpa.

Norm pulled a face. "Because fish stink and they've got stinky fish breath. **Obviously**."

Grandpa's eyes crinkled slightly in the corners. "I meant **why** don't you want to play a proper game of football?"

"Oh, right," said Norm. "Because I've got better things to do."

"Really?" said Grandpa. "Such as?"

Norm looked at Grandpa. Was he serious? Pretty much **anything** was better than playing **football.** Where did he even start? Because once he started they'd be there all flipping night!

As it happened, Norm didn't actually **have** to start. Because at that precise moment a car pulled up outside the house and a couple of doors slammed. It could only mean one thing. His mum and dad were back from parents' evening.

"I'd better get to bed, Grandpa."

Grandpa looked surprised. "Really? But your **brothers** aren't even in bed yet!"

"Yeah, I know," said Norm. "But I'm dead tired all of a sudden."

Norm yawned and stretched theatrically. Possibly a little bit **too** theatrically. Grandpa's eyes immediately crinkled in the corners again.

"What?" said Norm.

"What do you mean, what?" said Grandpa. "What's going on?"

"Nothing," said Norm scrambling to get under the duvet. "I just want to get to bed, that's all."

"Obviously."

"Uh?" said Norm.

"Well, you've still got all your clothes on," said Grandpa.

The front door slammed. Footsteps could be heard in the hall, heading for the stairs.

"Quick, Grandpa!" hissed Norm. "Go!"

"I beg your pardon?" said Grandpa.

"No offence," said Norm.

Grandpa studied Norm for a moment. "You don't want to see your parents, do you?"

"Whatever makes you think that, Grandpa?" said Norm. "Switch the light off on your way out."

"What do you say?"

"Please?" said Norm, disappearing beneath the duvet.

Grandpa shook his head but nevertheless got up and did as Norm asked. Stepping out onto the landing he came face to face with Norm's mum.

"Hello, Dad. Everything all right?"

"Ssshh!" said Grandpa.
"He's asleep."

"Who is?"

"Norman."

Shhhh

"Norman?" said
Norm's mum.

"He was exhausted,"
said Grandpa. "Must
be his hormones."

"Well, from what I've been hearing, it's definitely not from **working** too hard," said Norm's mum.

"Gordon flipping Bennet," muttered Norm from beneath the duvet.

"Norman?" said Norm's mum.

Oops, thought Norm. What should he do now? Pretend to snore? Start breathing heavily? Or just lie there and hope they'd go away?

"Must've been sleep-talking," said Grandpa.

"Hmmm," said Norm's mum.

"Cup of tea?"

"Go on then."

Good old Grandpa, thought Norm as he listened to two sets of footsteps padding downstairs. It looked like he owed him one.

CHAPTER 13

Grandpa saving Norm's bottom the previous night was merely delaying the inevitable the following morning and Norm knew it. It wasn't a question of **if** his parents brought the subject of the punishment exercise up – but **when**. Grandpa had bought Norm some extra time, that was all. And for that, Norm was extremely grateful. But now it looked like that time was very nearly up.

"Good sleep, love?" said Norm's mum as she stood by the sink, preparing the day's packed lunches.

"Yes, thanks," said Norm between mouthfuls of own-brand coco pops.

"You certainly had enough of it."

Norm laughed nervously. "Yeah. I was really tired last night, Mum. Dunno what came over me."

"Hmmm, well I think *I* might," said Norm's mum.

"Really, Mum?"

"Anything you'd like to ask?"

"What?" said Norm.

"Anything you'd like to ask?"

Norm knew **exactly** what his mum meant – but preferred to pretend that he didn't.

"Erm, what kind of sandwiches are you making?"

"Cheese and tomato. Same as always. Anything else?"

"Some mayo would be nice," said Norm.

Norm's mum sighed. "I meant anything else you'd like to **ask?**"

"Right," said Norm.

"Well?" said Norm's mum. "Is there?"

This was it then, thought Norm. He couldn't put it off any longer. Much as he'd like to. And anyway what was the big deal? He'd fallen asleep in history. So flipping what? It wasn't like he'd **wet** himself in history. Or **worse**. And anyway it wasn't **his** fault he'd been tired. It was Miss Rogers' fault for not being more interesting.

"What was it like?" muttered Norm.

"What was what like, love?"

Norm looked at his mum for a moment. She was standing with her back to him, but he could tell by her voice that she was smiling.

"The parents' evening?"

"Oh, the parents' evening?" said Norm's mum. "Funny you should ask."

Is it? thought Norm taking another mouthful of coco pops. Because it didn't sound very funny to him. Quite the opposite, in fact. It sounded very **unfunny** to **him**.

"It was...it was...it was..."

Gordon flipping Bennet, thought Norm. Why didn't she just put him out of his misery? **What** was it?

"Interesting," said Norm's mum at long last.

"Really?" said Norm.

"Yes," said Norm's mum.

144

"In what way?"

"Hmmm...let me see now."

Enough was enough, thought Norm. If **she** wasn't going to say it, **he** flipping would.

"If it's about the punishment exercise, I can explain everything, Mum."

Norm's mum stopped what she was doing and turned around.

"Punishment exercise? What punishment exercise?"

Norm stared open-mouthed.

"You're kidding, right? You **did** know?"

"Of course I knew," said Norm's mum.

Norm breathed a huge sigh of relief. It was bad enough that his mum and dad had to find out. But at least **he** hadn't been the one to tell them.

"So go on, then," said Norm's mum. "Explain."

Norm shrugged. "There's not a lot to explain. I fell asleep. I got a puni. End of."

"That's not what I heard, love."

Norm was genuinely surprised. "What? But..."

"I heard you gave your teacher a bit of backchat as well?"

Norm sniggered as he recalled the conversation.

"What?" said Norm's mum.

"Well, it was quite funny actually," said Norm.

"I don't care, Norman!" said Norm's mum. "You've got to pack that in!"

"Whatever," said Norm.

"There you go again!"

"What?"

"That's **exactly** what I mean!"

"Is there a problem here?" said Norm's dad walking into the kitchen.

"No, Dad," said Norm.

"Sure?"

"Sure, Dad."

Norm's mum and dad exchanged glances.

"He knows," said Norm's mum.

"Knows what?" said Norm's dad.

"That we know," said Norm's mum.

Norm's dad looked at Norm. "And?"

Norm was getting more confused by the second.

"Have you got something to say, Norman?"

"About, what?" said Norm.

"The punishment exercise?"

"Oh, right. That."

"Yes," said Norm's dad. "That."

"Erm…"

"Well?"

"Sorry," said Norm.

"Sorry?"

Norm nodded.

"Is that **all?**"

"Erm," said Norm. "It won't happen again?"

Norm's dad fixed Norm with a fierce glare.

"Are you **asking** me – or **telling** me?"

Norm thought for a moment. "Telling you?"

"Hmmm," said Norm's dad. "Well, it had better not."

Why? thought Norm. What would his dad do if it **did** happen again? Punish him? For getting a punishment exercise? Because **that** would be ri-flipping-diculous!

"Why did you fall asleep in class?" said Norm's dad.

Gordon flipping Bennet, thought Norm. Not **this** again? Why did his dad **think** he'd fallen asleep?

Gordon flipping Bennet

"I was tired, Dad."

"**Norman?**" said Norm's mum.

"What?" said Norm.

"What was I just **saying?**"

"Well, I **was** tired, Mum!"

"Yes, but **why** were you tired, Norman?" said Norm's dad.

"'Cos my bike's rubbish," muttered Norm. "Well, it **was**, anyway."

Norm's dad frowned until the lines on his forehead resembled a mini ploughed field.

"Pardon?"

"I was looking at new bikes on my iPad, Dad."

"And **that's** why you fell asleep in class the next day?"

Norm shrugged. "Pretty much, yeah."

No one said anything for a few seconds. Was that it? wondered Norm. Were his parents done banging on about stuff? Because if so there was something he needed to ask.

"Erm, don't suppose you…"

"What?" said Norm's dad.

"Mentioned my bike to the head teacher?"

"No, we did **not!**" snapped Norm's dad, the vein on the side of his head beginning to throb. Not that Norm noticed.

Throb
Throb

"But…"

"But **nothing**, Norman!" said Norm's dad. "I can't believe you've even got the nerve to ask!"

"Have you done it yet, love?" said Norm's mum ,stepping in to try and diffuse the situation.

"Done what, Mum?"

"The punishment exercise."

"Er, not yet, Mum, no."

"Well, make sure you do."

Norm nodded. But all he wanted to do now was finish his own-brand coco pops and get off to school as quickly as possible. Not that Norm particularly **wanted** to get to school quickly. He didn't particularly **want** to get to school at **all**. But anything was better than being stuck in the kitchen, with his mum and dad bombarding him with stupid questions. Or so he thought.

"You ready yet, boys?" called Norm's dad.

"YEAH!" yelled Brian and Dave stampeding down the stairs like a couple of elephants.

"Right. In the car then!"

"Gordon flipping Bennet," muttered Norm, suddenly realising that not only was he going to have to be driven to school by his dad again – he was going to have to share the car with his smelly little brothers again too.

"Is there a problem, Norman?" said Norm's dad.

Norm sighed. "No, Dad."

"Excellent. In the car then. Quick as you can now."

"Bye, love," said Norm's mum as Norm got up from the table and began trudging wearily towards the hall.

"Bye, Mum."

"Have a nice day."

"Yeah, right," muttered Norm under his breath.

"What was that, love?"

"Er, I said yeah, I **might,** Mum," said Norm, disappearing out the door.

CHAPTER 14

As things turned out, the drive to school **wasn't** as bad as Norm expected. It was even **worse**. Not only did his brothers quite literally not stop talking for a single second, his dad insisted on singing along to the radio pretty much the entire journey at the top of his goose-like voice. The combined racket was unbelievable. But at least it meant that Norm didn't have to say anything himself and could just stare out the window. Which was fine by Norm. The **last** thing he wanted to do was have to **talk** to Brian and Dave. And the less he spoke to his dad, the better as far as he was concerned.

It really was quite incredible, thought Norm. His brothers weren't so much talking **to** each other as talking **at** each other. There didn't appear to be any gaps at all in the conversation. How could they keep it up? How could they actually **breathe?** And what were they talking **about?** Because as far as Norm could tell, it was just a stream of non-stop drivel. Not that Norm actually **wanted** to listen. He did his best to tune out. But it was proving virtually impossible.

"SHUT UP!" yelled Norm, when it eventually got too much to bear.

That did it. Everything suddenly went very quiet in the car. Even the song on the radio ended.

"Daaaaaaad!" wailed Brian from the back seat. "Norman just told you to shut up!"

"What?" said Norm utterly horrified. "No, I didn't! I told **you** to shut up, Brian, you little freak!"

Dave giggled.

"**And** you!" said Norm.

"Charming," said Dave.

"Come on, guys," said Norm's dad. "At least *try* and get on."

"I'll try, Dad!" chirped Brian.

"Me too, Dad!" trilled Dave.

"Creeps," muttered Norm.

"Daaaaaaad!" wailed Brian. "Norman just called us 'creeps'!"

"Well, *that* went well," said Norm's dad. "Thanks a lot, guys."

"You're welcome," said Brian.

"I think he's being sarcastic, Brian," said Dave.

"Oh," said Brian.

Norm couldn't help sniggering.

"Something funny, Norman?" said Norm's dad.

"Er, no," said Norm. "I was just..."

"Just what?"

"Thinking of something."

"What?" said Norm's dad. "I could do with a laugh."

Norm thought for a moment. It was way too much effort to try and come up with anything vaguely witty and intelligent. Much easier to be like Grandpa and just say the first thing that popped into his head.

"Farting."

"You were thinking of farting?" said Norm's dad. "Could you at least open your window first?"

"What?"

said Norm. "No, Dad. I wasn't thinking of actually **farting**. I was just thinking that farting's funny, that's all."

"Really?" said Norm's dad. "You think **farting's** funny?"

Norm shrugged. "Doesn't everybody?"

"Honestly, Norman," said Dave. "You're so immature sometimes."

"Shut up, Dave," said Norm.

"Anyway, Norman, you shouldn't say 'fart'," said Brian.

"Uh?" said Norm.

"It's rude."

"What **should** I say then, Brian? Bottom burp? Trouser cough? Duvet hoverer?"

"I think you'll find the **correct** term is breaking wind," said Brian.

Trouser cough
Bottom burp
Duvet hoverer

Gordon flipping Bennet, thought Norm. There was only so much more of this he could take. He wasn't sure **how** much, exactly. But however much it was, it wasn't much.

"Dad?" said Dave when they'd driven on in silence for a few more seconds.

"Yes, Dave?"

"Are you going to be in the house today?"

Norm glanced at his little brother in the rear-view mirror. What kind of stupid question was **that?** Of **course** his dad was going to be in the flipping house today! His dad was **always** in the flipping house – and had been ever since he'd gone and got himself flipping sacked!

"Why do you ask?" said Norm's dad.

"In case a parcel gets delivered," said Dave.

"You **expecting** a parcel?"

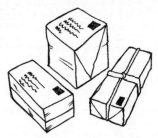

"My goalie gloves and shirt," said Dave.

Brilliant, thought Norm. Just what he flipping needed. Yet another reminder of just how unfair life was. Well, how unfair **his** life was anyway.

"That's a point," said Brian. "My Warhammer stuff might come today, Dad."

"What?" said Norm.

"My Warhammer stuff," said Brian.

"What Warhammer stuff?"

"The Great Beast of Gorgoroth," said Brian.

"Uh?" said Norm.

"*Lord of the Rings*," said Brian. "Mum saw it on one of the shopping channels."

"Yeah, but..."

"What?" said Brian.

"How come you're getting it?"

"Dunno," said Brian. "I think it was on special offer, or something."

Norm closed his eyes and took a deep breath. First he discovers that Dave is having something bought for him for no reason whatso-flipping-ever and now he finds out that Brian is, too? What about him? What was *he* getting? Apart from flipping angry? Abso-flipping-lutely nothing! It was the final straw. He couldn't contain his frustration any longer. He didn't even bother *trying* to contain his frustration any longer. It all suddenly came pouring out in one long, agonising scream.

AAAAAAAAAAAAARGH!!!

Norm opened his eyes again, only to discover that they'd stopped at some traffic lights and that several pedestrians were looking at him with rather quizzical expressions on their faces. All, that is, except for one, who was grinning from ear to ear and waving furiously in Norm's direction. Even above the sound of the engine there was no mistaking the voice. There never flipping was.

"Hello, **Norman!**" said Chelsea, deliberately overemphasising Norm's name like she always did. Like it was the funniest thing she'd ever heard.

Norm sighed. What was that about Brian getting something bought for him being the **final** straw? Wrong. **This** was the final straw. Or at least so Norm thought.

"OOOH YEAH, BABY!" screeched Norm's dad, suddenly bursting into song. "BABY, BABY, BABY! I LOVE YOU SOOOOOOOO!"

Great, thought Norm. If **yesterday** had been humiliating, **this** was humiliating with flipping knobs on! It was almost as if dad and brothers had got together with Chelsea beforehand and planned the whole flipping thing. And knowing **his** luck, thought Norm, they probably flipping **had!**

CHAPTER 15

The one good thing about Chelsea living next door with her dad – and there **was** only **one** good thing as far as Norm was concerned – was that she only lived there at weekends. The rest of the time she lived with her mum in a completely different part of town. In an ideal world, of course, she wouldn't have lived in a completely different **part** of town – she'd have lived in a completely different **town** altogether. But as Norm knew only too well, it **wasn't** an ideal world. His morning so far had been anything **but** ideal. Even **before** he'd seen Chelsea.

As Norm dawdled slowly into school, he seriously began to wonder. What was the actual **point** of Chelsea? What did she actually do, apart from get on his nerves and bug the heck out of him at every possible opportunity? She must do **something** else, thought Norm. But what? And how come she always popped up when he least **wanted** her to? It was as if she was monitoring his every move on CCTV cameras – or had some kind of special app on her phone to keep track of exactly where he was. How else would she have known to be at the lights just now? She didn't even go to the same flipping school! It was almost like she'd gone out of her **way** to humiliate him.

"In your own time then, Norman," said Miss Rogers when Norm eventually walked into class.

"What?" said Norm distractedly.

"You're late."

"Am I?"

There were a few isolated giggles. Norm looked around. There was only one desk without somebody sitting behind it. Everyone was looking at him.

"This is precisely what I was talking to your parents about," said Miss Rogers.

"Uh?" said Norm.

"**Pardon**," said Miss Rogers.

"Er, nothing," said Norm. "I just said, **uh?**"

Miss Rogers sighed. "I **heard** you the first time, Norman. What I meant was, the word is **pardon**. Not **uh?**"

"Pardon?"

"**Uh** is not a real word," said Miss Rogers.

Uh? thought Norm. Since when?

"This...attitude of yours has got to stop."

Norm pulled a face. "What attitude?"

"**That** attitude!" said Miss Rogers sharply.

"Uh?" said Norm. "I mean, what? I mean, pardon?"

There were a few more giggles.

"Do you **want** to be known as the class joker?" said Miss Rogers. "Is that it?"

Norm thought for a moment. **Did** he want to be known as the class joker? He wouldn't mind. As long as he didn't have to wear a flipping clown costume.

This is to certify that *Norman* can hang up his coat

"You've really got to pull your socks up, Norman. This isn't primary school, you know. You don't get a certificate **here** for learning how to hang your coat up or being **nice** to someone."

Norm didn't say anything. Partly because he didn't know **what** to say – but mainly because he wasn't sure whether Miss Rogers had actually finished or not. Teachers – and adults in general – tended to ramble on, in Norm's experience. It was usually best to just let them until they'd definitely stopped.

Miss Rogers regarded Norm quizzically. "How did you sleep last night?"

"Erm, OK."

"So you're not thinking of having a little nap, then?"

Norm sighed. There was nothing he would have liked **better** than to have had a little nap. Well, apart from having a great **big** nap and basically sleeping through the entire school day until it was time to go home again. But that wouldn't be allowed. And besides, he hadn't brought his toothbrush.

"Which reminds me," said Miss Rogers. "Where is it?"

"Where's what?" said Norm. "My toothbrush?"

That did it. Everyone burst out laughing.

"Your punishment exercise!" said Miss Rogers.

Oops, thought Norm. What with one thing and another, he **still** hadn't flipping done it.

"Well?" said Miss Rogers. "I'm waiting."

"Erm…"

"You **have** done it, haven't you, Norman?"

"Er, not exactly," said Norm.

"Not exactly?" said Miss Rogers. "Have you, or haven't you?"

"No," said Norm.

Miss Rogers sighed. "In that case you leave me no alternative."

This wasn't sounding good, thought Norm. This wasn't sounding good at all.

"I'm afraid I'm going to have to double it."

"Wha..." began Norm. "I mean, pardon?"

"You heard," said Miss Rogers. "You've just earned yourself **another** punishment exercise on **top** of the one you haven't done."

Gordon flipping Bennet, thought Norm. And to think it was still only first flipping period! Today really was turning into a bit of a nightmare! What **else** was going to happen?

"I must say I'm very disappointed, Norman."

Norm looked at Miss Rogers for a second. She was disappointed? How did she think **he** felt?

"This is hardly the fresh start I was hoping for."

"Yeah, but..."

"Did your parents not tell you about our little chat last night?"

Punishment exercise no. 2

"Yeah, but..."

"What, Norman?" said Miss Rogers.

It was a good question actually, thought Norm. What? There was no point trying to argue. If he did, there was every chance she'd treble it and before he knew it he'd have **three**

Punishment exercise no. 1

flipping punishment exercises instead of one! No, thought Norm. He was just going to have to bite his tongue and take it, no matter **how** outrageous and unfair he might think it was.

"Well?" said Miss Rogers.

Norm sighed. "Nothing."

"Excellent," said Miss Rogers. "In that case, you can sit down."

As Norm made his way to the one free desk, he happened to catch Connor Wright's eye.

"Oh well," he said. "Things can only get better."

"Ha," snorted Norm. "You wanna flipping bet?"

CHAPTER 16

"All right, Norm?" said Mikey when the pair met in the playground that lunchtime.

"No, I'm flipping not, actually," muttered Norm darkly.

"Why not?" said Mikey.

Norm sighed. "How long have you got?"

Mikey looked at his watch. "About half an hour."

Half a flipping hour? thought Norm. That wasn't **nearly** long enough. Not if he **really** wanted to let rip and vent **all** his frustrations.

Which was probably what he needed to do right now. And who better to actually vent all his frustrations **to** than his lifelong best friend, Mikey?

"Well?" said Mikey expectantly. "I'm waiting."

Norm sighed again. "Where do I start?"

"How about the beginning?"

The beginning? thought Norm. How far back did Mikey actually **mean?** To when he was a baby? To when he and Mikey first met at parent and toddler group? To when Brian and Dave were born? This could take some time. He might just have to fast forward through all the boring bits.

"Hi, guys," said a cheery voice.

Gordon flipping Bennet, thought Norm turning round to see Connor Wright making a beeline for them. What did **he** want? Again! And how come he was **so** flipping cheerful? Didn't he realise how incredibly irritating that was? Obviously not.

"How's it going?"

"Not good," said Mikey.

"Hmm, well I'm not surprised," said Connor Wright. "I thought that was bang out of order by the way."

Mikey pulled a face. "What was?"

"Being given another punishment exercise."

"**Another** one?" said Mikey. "So **that's** why you're not all right, Norm."

"Yeah," mumbled Norm. "Amongst other things."

"Right," said Connor Wright. "Still no sign of your bike, then?"

"What do **you** think?" said Norm.

"Sorry," said Connor Wright. "That must be really annoying."

"What?" said Norm. "That my bike's been nicked?"

"No," said Connor Wright. "Well, I mean, yeah. Obviously. But what I mean is it must be really annoying, people **asking** you about it all the time?"

"It is a bit, yeah," said Norm. "Actually it is a **lot.**"

"It's kind of a big deal to Norm," said Mikey.

"His bike?" said Connor Wright. "Yeah, I know it is."

"No, but I mean it's like, a really big deal," said Mikey. "He wants to be World Mountain Biking Champion."

Norm turned to Mikey.

"I **am** here you know."

"What?" said Mikey.
"I know you are, Norm."

"I **can** speak for myself."

"Sorry," said Mikey.

"I think that's great," said Connor Wright.

"What is?" said Norm. "That I can speak for myself?"

"No. That you want to be World Mountain Biking Champion."

Norm pulled a face. "Really?"

Connor Wright nodded.

"But..."

"What? I called you a geek for liking bikes?"

Norm shrugged. "Well, yeah. Basically."

Connor Wright looked sheepish. "I told you on Facebook. I didn't actually **mean** it. I was joking."

Norm thought for a moment, unsure whether to believe Connor Wright or not. Unsure whether it actually **mattered** if he believed Connor Wright or not. Unsure whether he even **cared** one way or the other. All that Norm cared about was his bike and what had happened to it. If only there was some way of finding out. If only there was something he could **do**. Then at least he'd have something to say the next time someone flipping **asked** him about it!

"Talking of Facebook," said Connor Wright.

"Were we?" said Norm.

"Have you thought about mentioning it?"

"Mentioning what? Facebook?"

"No!" said Connor Wright. "Mentioning your **bike** on Facebook!"

"Actually that's a really good idea, Norm!" said Mikey. "You could post a photo! Loads of people would see it! It could go viral!"

"Yeah," said Connor Wright. "My dad lost his car keys once and posted something about it on Facebook and he got them back in, like, an hour or something."

Well, whoopee flipping do, thought Norm. Good for Connor Wright's dad. Didn't mean it would work for **him**, though, did it? Maybe it had just been Connor Wright's dad's lucky day? Maybe all the planets had been lined up or whatever it was that flipping planets were supposed to do. Maybe a black cat had crossed in front of him or something. Whatever, thought Norm. If luck was going to play any part in getting his bike back he could flipping well forget it. Because **he** hardly **ever** had lucky days! And one thing was for sure. This wasn't one of them!

"Why didn't **you** think of that, Norm?" said Mikey.

"How do you know I **hadn't** thought of it?" said Norm.

Mikey looked at Norm. "**Had** you?"

Norm shrugged. "Maybe."

"Actually," said Connor Wright, "there **is** one more thing we could try."

We? thought Norm. What did he mean, we? He couldn't remember asking Connor Wright to help look for his bike. Then again, thought Norm, there were days when he could scarcely remember getting out of bed, let alone getting dressed. So maybe he **had** asked.

"Do you want me to tell you?"

Norm sighed. "Go on, then."

"Well, there's this guy I know," said Connor Wright.

"Yeah?" said Norm. "So what?"

"Well, **he** knows someone."

Was there actually going to be a point to this story? wondered Norm. Connor Wright **knew** someone who knew someone? That was a bit like finding out that all vegetables were essentially evil. Or that water was wet. It wasn't exactly earth-shattering news.

"Anyway," said Connor Wright, carrying on regardless. "**That** someone might know someone who might know something."

Gordon flipping Bennet, thought Norm. This was seriously beginning to do his nut in. What on **earth** was Connor Wright going on about? Because to be perfectly honest he'd **completely** lost track of who knew who and who might do what.

"So this guy you know who **knows** someone might **know** someone else?" said Mikey.

"Yeah," said Connor Wright.

"And **that** someone might know something about Norm's **bike?**"

"Exactly!" said Connor Wright.

"Do you see what he means, Norm?" said Mikey.

"What?" said Norm. "Course I see what he means, you doughnut! I'm not actually **stupid!**"

"I know you're not," said Mikey.

"So why flipping ask, then?" said Norm.

"So anyway," said Connor Wright, stepping in. "I was wondering if…"

"What?"

"You'd like me to have a word?"

Norm pulled a face. "Who with?"

"The guy I know who knows someone who might know someone who might know something?"

Hmm, thought Norm. **Would** he like Connor Wright to have a word? He'd got nothing to lose. Not any more he hadn't. He'd already **lost** his bike. How much worse could it actually get?

"Well?" said Connor Wright. "Would you?"

Norm shrugged. "Can if you want."

"I'd like to," said Connor Wright.

"You'd **like** to?" said Norm. "Why? What's in it for you?"

Mikey looked shocked. "Norm!"

"What?"

"He's just trying to be **helpful**. It doesn't mean he wants anything in **return**."

Norm considered this for a few moments. Maybe Mikey was right. Perhaps he **was** being a bit harsh on Connor Wright. Perhaps Connor Wright really **wasn't** after anything. Perhaps Norm had got him all wrong.

"Sorry," said Norm.

Connor Wright smiled. "That's OK. It's no biggie."

Norm wasn't sure what else to say. The truth was he was beginning to feel just ever so slightly guilty. He clearly **had** misjudged Connor Wright's motives. He was obviously just being nice.

"Now you come to mention it though..."

"What?"

"There **is** something you could do," said Connor Wright.

Norm sighed. "I flipping **knew** it!"

"Give him a chance, Norm!" said Mikey. "You don't know what he's going to say yet!"

"Thank you, Mikey," said Connor Wright.

"You're welcome," said Mikey.

"Well?" said Norm expectantly. "I'm all ears."

Connor Wright looked Norm straight in the eyes. "You changed your mind yet?"

Norm looked puzzled. "About what?"

"Playing football tomorrow?"

"Uh?" said Norm. "Never mind *that.* What's in it for you if you have a word about my bike with that guy?"

Connor Wright continued to look straight at Norm and raised his eyebrows. "Guess."

"Erm, Norm?" said Mikey hesitantly.

"What?" snapped Norm.

"I *think* what Connor's trying to say is that if *you* play football tomorrow, *he'll* have a word about your bike with the guy who knows someone who might know someone who might know something. Is that right, Connor?"

Connor Wright nodded. "Pretty much, yeah."

Gordon flipping Bennet, thought Norm. Was Connor Wright *ever* going to stop banging on about this flipping football match, or what? He just didn't flipping get it, did he? He *hated* football! Or strongly disliked it, or whatever. No, actually, thought Norm, he was right the first time. He **hated** football. The question was – did he hate it enough that he wouldn't agree to play even if there **was** a chance of getting his bike back? Even a teensy chance? Even a **really** teensy chance?

"Connor!" yelled a voice from over by the football pitch. "You coming, or what?"

"In a minute!" yelled Connor Wright before turning back to Norm. "You don't need to decide now."

Thank goodness for **that**, thought Norm.

"I'll message you later," said Connor Wright, heading off.

"Take your time," muttered Norm, watching him go.

"What are you going to do, Norm?" said Mikey.

It was a good question, thought Norm. What **was** he going to do?

CHAPTER 17

There was only one person who could possibly help Norm decide whether to play football the next

day or not. Well, as far as **Norm** was concerned there was, anyway. It was the same person Norm **always** went to whenever he felt he had the weight of the world on his shoulders. Or, in other words, most of the time.

"Hi, Grandpa."

"Hi, yourself," said Grandpa emerging from his shed in the allotments, watering can in hand. "Still no sign of the bike, then?"

Norm bit his tongue and shook his head.

"That would explain it then."

"Explain what?" said Norm.

"Why you've got a face on you like a baboon's backside."

Norm thought for a moment. He wasn't sure he actually knew what a baboon's backside *looked* like. He wasn't sure he actually *wanted* to, either.

"How long's it been, now?" said Grandpa filling the watering can from a tap sticking out of the ground.

Norm sighed. "Two days."

"Two days?" said Grandpa. "Is that all?"

Norm was gobsmacked. Was that **all?** Two days might not seem like very long to Grandpa, but it seemed like a whole flipping **lifetime** to him. **Especially** without a bike!

"I remember once when I was your age…"

Norm waited for Grandpa to continue. But he didn't.

"What, Grandpa?"

"Eh?"

"What do you remember when you were my age?"

Grandpa thought for a moment. "It'll come to me in a second."

Norm couldn't help smiling. This was why it was so good spending time with Grandpa. Even if he couldn't always offer a practical solution, it was better than letting things stew and bubble away in his head like some kind of emotional stew. And besides, **anything** was better than being at home listening to his parents droning on – or his flipping brothers babbling away like a pair of demented chipmunks.

"So what are you doing about it?"

"About what?" said Norm.

"Your **bike!**" said Grandpa.

"Oh, right," said Norm.

"You can't just expect it to magically **reappear,** Norman. You need to actually **do** something."

"Erm, well I'm thinking about posting something about it on Facebook."

"**Thinking** about it?" said Grandpa.

"Yeah," said Norm.

"It's no good just **thinking** about it," said Grandpa.

Norm knew Grandpa was right. Not only that, Grandpa **knew** that Norm knew he was right. Not only that, Norm knew that Grandpa knew that Norm knew he was right.

"I'm **thinking** about doing a naked bungee jump for charity," said Grandpa.

Norm looked at Grandpa for a second – unsure whether or not this was some kind of wind-up. He flipping **hoped** so. But even if it was, this was an image that was likely to haunt Norm's imagination for some time to come.

"Please tell me you're not serious, Grandpa?"

"OK," said Grandpa.

Norm was getting confused. "What do you mean, OK?"

"I mean I'm not serious."

"Thank goodness for **that**," muttered Norm.

"I'm not going to do it for charity," said Grandpa.

"What?" said Norm.

"I'm just going to do it for a laugh."

"But..."

Grandpa's eyes immediately began to crinkle ever so slightly in the corners.

"Sorry, Norman. Couldn't resist it. The point is..."

Once again Norm waited for Grandpa to continue.

But once again Grandpa didn't.

"Grandpa?"

"Yes?"

"You were saying?"

Grandpa pulled a face. "Was I? Oh yes, I was, wasn't I? So are you doing it, or not?"

"Doing what?" said Norm.

"Posting something about your bike on Facepage?"

"Book."

"Pardon?"

"It's not **Facepage**, Grandpa," said Norm. "It's **Facebook**."

"I couldn't give a flying squirrel what it's called,

Norman. Are you going to do it, or not?"

Norm nodded. "Yep."

"Definitely?"

"**Definitely**," said Norm.

"Is the **correct** answer!" said Grandpa with a flourish, as if he was the host of a TV quiz show.

Norm suddenly remembered Connor Wright's offer. Or deal. Or whatever you wanted to call it. Should he tell Grandpa about **that** as well? Why not? It couldn't do any harm.

"Also, there's this guy I know..."

"Fascinating," said Grandpa, cutting Norm off before he could finish. "Now, if you'll just excuse me, I've got work to do."

Norm pulled a face. "What?"

"This watering can's not just for show, you know."

"But…"

"What?" said Grandpa beginning to water a row of cabbages. Not that Norm actually **_knew_** they were a row of cabbages. As far as **_Norm_** was concerned they were just a row of green things. And green things – as far as **_Norm_** was concerned – were generally things to be avoided. Unless they happened to be Haribos. That was different.

"I hadn't finished."

Grandpa exhaled noisily. "Go on then. But quick."

"Well, you see, there's this guy I know," began Norm.

"I know," said Grandpa. "You just told me."

"Yeah, I know I did," said Norm. "But you see, he knows someone who knows someone who **_might_** know someone who **might** know something about my bike!"

"I see," said Grandpa.

"Really?" said Norm doubtfully.

"Of course," said Grandpa. "You know someone who knows someone who might know someone who might know something about your bike. Simple."

"Whoa," said Norm.

"I've told you before, Norman. I'm not quite as daft as I look."

"Not **quite**," muttered Norm.

"And I'm not deaf, either," said Grandpa, carrying on watering the cabbages. Or as far as **Norm** was concerned, carrying on watering the row of green things.

"So?" said Grandpa eventually.

"What?" said Norm.

"Is this guy going to have a word, or what?"

Norm sighed. "There's a catch."

"Ah," said Grandpa, turning round and straightening up. "There usually is."

"Tell me about it," said Norm.

"Well, you see—"

"Grandpa?"

"What?"

"It's just an expression," said Norm. "I don't **really** want you to tell me about it. I **know** there's usually a catch."

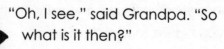

"Oh, I see," said Grandpa. "So what is it then?"

Norm sighed again. If anything

it was an even more heartfelt sigh than the last one. "He wants me to play football."

"Oh, *that* guy," said Grandpa. "The one you were telling me about last night?"

Norm nodded.

"What's his name again?"

"Connor Wright."

"That's right," said Grandpa.

Uh? thought Norm. Course he was flipping right. His memory wasn't *that* bad!

"So he's basically blackmailing you, then?"

"What?" said Norm.

"He's going to have a word with this guy he knows *if* you agree to play football?"

"Pretty much, yeah," said Norm.

"And let me guess. You'd sooner snog a haddock?"

"A halibut, actually," said Norm.

"Same thing," said Grandpa. "The point is you don't want to play."

Norm shook his head.

"Hmm," said Grandpa. "You know, you might want to think about that."

"Hang on a minute, Grandpa."

"What?"

"I'm thinking about it right now," said Norm, furrowing his brow and stroking his chin thoughtfully.

"And?" said Grandpa.

"Still don't want to play," said Norm.

Grandpa resumed watering the cabbages. Or as far as Norm was concerned, he resumed watering the row of green things.

"Did I ever tell you about the time *I* got picked to play for the school, Norman?"

"You mean for the football team?"

"No, said Grandpa. "The synchronised knitting team."

"Uh?" said Norm.

"Of *course* I mean the football team, you numpty."

"Oh, right," said Norm. "And?"

"Well, that's the thing."

What was the thing? wondered Norm. Grandpa couldn't keep leaving him hanging on like this. It was beginning to get *seriously* annoying. And if there was one thing Norm **didn't** need right now, it was something **else** that was seriously annoying. But this time, Grandpa **did** continue...

"I didn't play."

"Why not, Grandpa?"

"I'm not sure," said Grandpa. "I think I went to see a movie. There was probably a girl involved, too."

Norm was horrified. A **girl?** Grandpa might as well have said there was a flipping **llama** involved.

"I can't remember, to be perfectly honest," said Grandpa. "It was a long time ago."

Yes, thought Norm, a **very** long time ago. And this was all very interesting, but what had it got to do with **him**?

Where was it all leading? Was it actually leading **anywhere?**

Grandpa sighed. "What I **can** remember is the feeling of regret afterwards."

"Regret?" said Norm.

Grandpa nodded. "And ever since."

"What do you mean, Grandpa?"

Grandpa straightened up and turned around again.

"What I mean, Norman, is..."

Grandpa stopped midsentence and stared wistfully into the distance. Norm looked to try and work out what exactly it was that Grandpa was staring **at** – but all that he could see was a bus, passing the allotments. What was so interesting about a flipping bus? Not a lot, decided Norm.

"Are you OK, Grandpa?"

"Yes, yes, of course. I was just thinking, that's all."

"What about?" said Norm.

Grandpa sighed. "What might have been."

Gordon flipping Bennet, thought Norm. It was beginning to feel like he was in a play, or a flipping **book** or something! What was Grandpa on about? Feelings of flipping regret and what might have flipping been? What was this? Flipping Victorian times, or something?

"But it's no good dwelling on the past, Norman."

No, thought Norm. So let's not flipping bother.

"What's done is done," said Grandpa. "It's all water under the bridge now."

Norm nodded, even though he hadn't the faintest idea what Grandpa was on about.

"And anyway," said Grandpa, "how was I to know what would happen?"

Norm watched as Grandpa began heading back towards his shed. He clearly wasn't about to elaborate any further. And now Norm's curiosity had got the better of him. It was **SO** flipping annoying.

"Grandpa?"

Grandpa stopped and turned to face Norm.

"What is it?"

"Well?" said Norm

"Well, what?"

Norm sighed. "What *did* happen?"

"Nothing, as far as I know," said Grandpa. "But that's not the point, Norman. The point is..."

"What?" said Norm.

"I think you should do it."

Norm was confused. "Do *what?*"

"Play," said Grandpa.

"Football?"

Grandpa nodded. "For me."

"Uh?" said Norm, who by now was even more confused. "I didn't even know you *had* a team, Grandpa!"

"What?" said Grandpa. "No, I don't mean actually play for me, you numpty!"

"What, then?" said Norm.

"I mean *do* it for me," said Grandpa. "To make me happy."

"But..."

"I might not be around much longer."

Whoa, thought Norm. Had Grandpa really just said what Norm *thought* he'd just said? Or rather, had Grandpa really just **meant** what Norm *thought* he'd just meant? There was only one way of knowing.

"You mean you're going *out,* Grandpa?"

"Not exactly, no," said Grandpa. "Or at least if I **am**, I might not be coming back again."

Right, thought Norm. Well that was fairly conclusive then.

"You do understand, don't you?" said Grandpa.

Norm nodded. Not only did he now fully understand what Grandpa had meant, he felt it only polite to ask another question.

"When?"

Grandpa shrugged. "Who knows? Could be any time."

Norm was beginning to wish he hadn't bothered coming to the allotments after all. If he'd known the conversation was going to be as depressing as this, he would have gone straight home and played on the Xbox instead.

"So?" said Grandpa. "Are you going to play, or not?"

Norm sighed. How could he **not** flipping play **now?** Now that Grandpa had said **that?** That if he **did** play it would make Grandpa flipping happy? What was he? Some kind of evil, feelingless **monster?** It was **so** flipping unfair!

"Well?" said Grandpa.

"Yeah, I'll play," said Norm.

"That's my boy," said Grandpa, his eyes crinkling ever so slightly in the corners. "And you never know..."

"What?" said Norm.

"You **might** just find out what's happened to your bike!"

Norm couldn't help smiling. What with all the talk of Grandpa seemingly about to kick the bucket any second now, he'd actually forgotten all 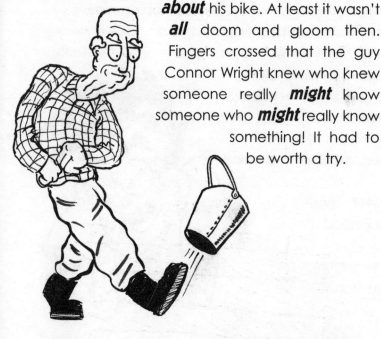 **about** his bike. At least it wasn't **all** doom and gloom then. Fingers crossed that the guy Connor Wright knew who knew someone really **might** know someone who **might** really know something! It had to be worth a try.

CHAPTER 18

As per usual, any faint ray of optimism Norm may have briefly felt was quickly extinguished the moment he got home. In fact any ray of optimism Norm **may** have briefly felt was extinguished even **before** he got home. It **was** Friday after all. Not that it particularly mattered **what** day of the week it was. **Every** day had the potential to suddenly go pear-shaped, as far as Norm was concerned. But on Fridays the potential was even greater than normal. And for one very good reason.

"Hello, **Norman!**" said Chelsea from the other side of the fence, the moment Norm set foot on his drive. "There's no one in!"

Gordon flipping Bennet, thought Norm. She could've at least waited till he'd changed out of his uniform and got himself a flipping snack! But no. She was straight in there, like a rat up a flipping drainpipe! And anyway, how did **she** know there was no one in?

"What's the matter, **Norman?** Not talking?"

What kind of stupid question was **that?** thought Norm. Did it **look** like he was flipping talking?

"Well?" said Chelsea.

Norm shrugged. "Nothing to say."

"Really?" said Chelsea. "That's funny. Because you seemed to have plenty to say this **morning!**"

Norm sighed. He hadn't even reached the front door yet, but already it felt as if his blood was beginning to boil, like molten lava in a volcano. This didn't bode well at all.

"Something wrong, was there?"

"What?" said Norm irritably.

"This morning?" said Chelsea. "When I saw you in your car?"

"Oh, that?" said Norm, recalling his scream of anguish on the school run. "That was just my brothers. They were driving me mad."

"Aw, how **could** they?" cooed Chelsea in a squeaky baby voice. "They're so sweeeeet!"

Norm snorted with derision. "You reckon? Try flipping **living** with them!"

"Now, now, **Norman!** There's no need for that!"

"Flipping well is," muttered Norm.

"Ooh, that reminds me," said Chelsea.

"What?"

"I've got something for you."

Norm pulled a face. "What?"

"Wait there a sec," said Chelsea disappearing.

Uh? thought Norm. Who on **earth** did she think she was – telling **him** to wait there a sec? On his own flipping drive! He'd wait there a sec if he flipping **wanted** to wait there a sec! Not because someone had **told** him to wait there a sec! Especially flipping Chelsea! What a flipping nerve! But by now it was too late anyway. Chelsea had already reappeared. And not on the other side of the fence either – but coming up the drive. It was **so** flipping annoying.

Norm stared, open-mouthed. Not only was Chelsea carrying a couple of parcels, he could now see that she was decked out in full football kit.

"What's the matter, **Norman?**"

"Erm..."

"Well?" said Chelsea. "Don't just stand there gawping like a goldfish!"

"Why are you dressed like that?"

"Seriously?"

Norm nodded.

"Because I've been playing football," said Chelsea. "I mean, duh!"

"Uh?" said Norm. "But..."

"What?" said Chelsea. "You didn't know girls played football?"

"No," said Norm.

"You're kidding me, right?"

"But..."

"What?" said Chelsea.

"I hadn't finished," said Norm.

"Go on then," said Chelsea.

"What I was **going** to say," said Norm, "was that I knew **girls** played football. I just didn't know **you** played football."

"Oh, right," said Chelsea.

"You said you didn't even **like** football."

"Did I?"

"Yeah," said Norm. "When I first met you."

Chelsea grinned.

"What's so funny about that?" said Norm before suddenly realising **exactly** what was so funny about that.

"You remember the first time you **met** me?"

"No," said Norm a bit too quickly. "I mean yeah. I mean maybe."

Chelsea laughed. "Make your mind up, **_Norman!_**"

Norm was quite certain about one thing. He wanted nothing more than for the earth to open up at that moment and swallow him whole. But it didn't. Instead, Chelsea just kept looking at him and grinning from ear to ear.

"I obviously made quite an impression on you."

Norm could feel himself beginning to blush. There was nothing he could do about it. It was **_beyond_** annoying.

"Why are you going red, Norman?"

"I'm not going red!"

"I think you'll find you are," said Chelsea. "Anyway, it's just a one-off."

Norm looked puzzled. What was just a one-off? Him going red? What was Chelsea on about?

"Me playing football," said Chelsea as if she'd read Norm's mind.

"Oh, right," said Norm.

"They were a man short," said Chelsea. "Or a girl, anyway."

"What are the odds?" muttered Norm.

"Of what?"

Norm shrugged. "Nothing."

"Oh, come on, **Norman**," said Chelsea. "Don't be such a tease. You've got me all intrigued now! What are the odds of **what?**"

Oh, what the heck? thought Norm. She was bound to find out **sooner** or later, just like she seemed to find out about everything else. He might as well tell her **now** and save flipping time.

"I've got a match tomorrow too."

Chelsea looked genuinely surprised. "Really? A **football** match?"

Norm nodded. "Just a one-off. **They're** a man short too."

Chelsea laughed again. "A **boy** short, don't you mean?"

"Ha, ha," sneered Norm. "Very funny."

"Like you say," said Chelsea. "What are the odds, eh?"

They looked at each other for a few seconds.

"Well?" said Chelsea.

"Are you actually going to **take** these parcels from me, or are you going to stare at me like I've just stepped off a spaceship?"

"Uh?" said Norm.

"I come in peace!" said Chelsea in a funny alien voice.

Norm sighed and took the parcels. He had a pretty good idea what they were.

"How come they were delivered to **your** house, anyway?"

"I told you," said Chelsea. "No one was in. So they were delivered to my dad's instead."

"Right," said Norm.

"Who are they for?"

Norm snorted. "Not **me** for a flipping start."

"Who then?" said Chelsea.

"My stupid little brothers."

"That's not very nice, **Norman**."

Norm shrugged. "Whatever."

"What are they?" said Chelsea.

Good question, thought Norm. What exactly **were** his brothers? Because until it was scientifically proven otherwise, he refused to believe that he could **possibly** be biologically related to either Brian or Dave.

"What are the **parcels?**" said Chelsea as if she'd read Norm's mind again.

"Oh, right," said Norm. "Just, you know..."

"No, I **don't** know actually, **Norman**. I'm not **psychic**, you know!"

"Could've fooled me."

"I knew you were going to say that," said Chelsea.

"What?" said Norm.

"Nothing," said Chelsea. "What's in the parcels?"

"Stuff."

"Stuff?" said Chelsea tilting her head and raising her eyebrows.

Gordon flipping Bennet, thought Norm. She was like a dog with a flipping bone. She just wouldn't let go!

"If you **must** know – goalie gloves and shirt for Dave and some nerdy *Lord of the Rings* stuff for **Brian**."

"See?" said Chelsea.

"What?" said Norm.

"That wasn't difficult, was it?"

Norm glared at Chelsea. How did **she** know how difficult it had been? **She** didn't have annoying brothers or sisters who got whatever they flipping wanted **whenever** they flipping wanted it. She was an only child – something which, right now, Norm desperately wished **he** was as well.

"What about you, **Norman?**"

"What about me?"

"How come you haven't got a parcel?"

Norm shrugged. "Dunno. Just haven't."

Chelsea pulled a face. "Bit unfair, isn't it?"

Norm snorted again. "A **bit?**"

"What have **you** done wrong?"

It was another good question, thought Norm. What had he done wrong? Abso-flipping-lutely **nothing** as far as **he** could see. But then Norm was perfectly used to massive miscarriages of justice. He was all too familiar with being blamed for

stuff he hadn't actually done. Only too aware that **everything** was just so flipping unfair. This was just par for the course. It was what he'd come to expect.

Chelsea regarded Norm for a moment and pursed her lips.

"What are you looking at me like that for?" said Norm.

"Nothing," said Chelsea. "Just thinking, that's all."

"What about?"

Chelsea seemed to hesitate.

"What?" said Norm.

"Have you got any kit?"

"Uh?" said Norm. "What kind of kit?"

"Football kit," said Chelsea. "For tomorrow?"

Norm thought for a second. Now Chelsea came to mention it, he **hadn't** got any football kit. He'd **never** had any **need** for any football kit. Why would he? He was more likely to need a deep sea diver's suit than he was to ever need a flipping football kit! Until now, anyway.

"Well?" said Chelsea.

"Erm, not really," said Norm.

"Not really?" said Chelsea. "Have you, or haven't you got any football kit, **Norman?**"

"No," said Norm.

"Hmm," said Chelsea thoughtfully. "Your brother's would obviously be too small."

"Obviously," said Norm.

"So what are you going to do about it?"

Norm thought for a moment. "Dunno."

"Hmm," said Chelsea again.

Hmm? thought Norm. What was flipping *hmm* supposed to mean? And why was Chelsea smiling like that?

"You know, you could always borrow mine."

Norm stared at Chelsea with a mixture of revulsion and utter incredulity. This just *had* to be a wind-up. She couldn't *possibly* be serious? Could she?

"What's wrong with that, *Norman?*"

What was *wrong* with it? wondered Norm. What was flipping *right* with it, more like? The mere *thought* of wearing something that *Chelsea* had previously worn was enough to make him want to throw up. It would be like...like...like...Norm stopped wondering what it would be like. It was too horrific to even think about.

"What size feet are you?"

"What?" said Norm.

"I'm only talking about lending you my **boots**," giggled Chelsea.

"What?" said Norm again.

"You didn't think I meant shorts and shirt as **well,** did you?"

"Erm, no. Course not!"

"'Cos that would be disgusting!" said Chelsea.

"Yeah, course," said Norm.

"And anyway, shorts and shirt will be provided," said Chelsea. "Obviously."

"Yeah, obviously," said Norm, pretending that he'd known that all along.

"So?" said Chelsea. "What size feet are you?"

"Erm, five, I think."

"What are the odds?" laughed Chelsea. "Me too!"

Norm laughed too. Partly because he didn't know what else to do – but mainly out of sheer relief. Compared to wearing Chelsea's shorts and shirt, the idea of just having to wear her **boots** suddenly didn't seem like **quite** such a horrific idea after all. Even if it **was** a bit embarrassing that he and a flipping **girl** had the same size feet. And anyway, where else was he going to get hold of any boots at this short notice? His skinflint parents certainly weren't going to cough up, that was for sure. And he couldn't play football in his plimsolls.

"Well?" said Chelsea. "Do you want to borrow them, or not?"

Norm nodded. "Yeah, all right then."

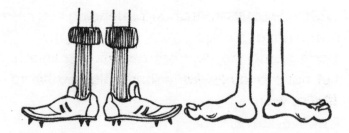

"Excellent," said Chelsea disappearing down the drive. "I'll bring them round later."

"'Kay," said Norm watching her go.

"You're welcome, by the way," said Chelsea.

"What?" said Norm, fishing in his school bag for the spare front door key.

"I said you're **welcome!**"

"Yeah, whatever," muttered Norm letting himself into the house.

"I heard that, **Norman**."

"Gordon flipping Bennet," muttered Norm.

"**And** I heard that," laughed Chelsea.

Norm closed the door behind him and sighed. But not too loudly, just in case Chelsea heard **that** as well.

CHAPTER 19

Norm wasn't alone in the house for very long. Within a couple of minutes, Brian and Dave had both burst in, yelling at the tops of their voices, followed by John, yapping at the top of his. Finally, Norm's mum walked into the kitchen, where Norm was already helping himself to a bag of supermarket own-brand crisps and a glass of supermarket own-brand cola.

"Hello, love."

"Oh hi, Mum," said Norm looking around.

"I do wish you'd ask first instead of just helping yourself."

Norm pulled a face. "But you weren't actually **_here_**, Mum. What was I supposed to do? Phone you, or something?"

"Now, now, love," said Norm's mum. "There's no need for that."

As far as Norm was concerned though, there was **_every_** need for that. But he decided not to say anything. He **_couldn't_** say anything anyway, because he'd just stuffed his mouth with another handful of crisps.

"How was school?"

Norm thought for a moment. How was school? Flipping rubbish, same as it always was. Would his mum and dad **_never_** learn?

"Well?" said Norm's mum expectantly.

Norm shrugged. "It was all right."

"Have you done that punishment exercise yet?"

Norm looked at his mum. Was this a good time to

mention that not only had he not done the punishment exercise he'd actually been given **another** one? Probably not.

"Not yet, Mum, no."

"Hmm," said Norm's mum.

"Where's Dad?" said Norm, keen to change the subject.

"Oh, didn't he tell you?" said Norm's mum.

Uh? thought Norm. Hadn't his dad told him **what?** Until he knew that, he had no **idea** whether he'd told him or not. His mum really did need to be a bit more specific sometimes.

"He's got an interview."

Uh? thought Norm again. Why would anyone want to interview his flipping dad? His dad wasn't famous. His dad was the most boring person he knew. He didn't have any particular talents or skills that Norm knew of. It would be like trying to interview a flipping

jellyfish. Except not quite as interesting.

"You mean, like…for a newspaper or a magazine or something?"

Norm's mum laughed. "No!"

"What, so you mean like on the **telly?**" said Norm growing more and more incredulous.

"Not **that** kind of interview!" said Norm's mum.

Norm was truly puzzled. "What kind then?"

"For a job."

Norm stared at his mum as if she'd just announced that she was running away to join a circus."A job?"

Norm's mum nodded.

"You mean like…"

Norm's mum nodded again. "A job, yes."

"Whoa," said Norm. "What for?"

"I'm afraid we need the money, love."

"What?" said Norm. "No, I meant, what *job* is the *interview* for?"

"Oh, I see," said Norm's mum. "I'm not actually sure."

Norm wasn't sure why he'd even bothered asking. He'd never really known what his dad's job was when he'd actually *had* one. Who cared what the job was, frankly? Norm certainly didn't. All that mattered was that his dad might soon be working again – and when that happened they'd be able to afford *proper* flipping crisps and *proper* flipping cola! There'd be none of that supermarket own-brand rubbish anymore.

"So when *are* you going to do it, then?" said Norm's mum.

"Do what?" said Norm distractedly.

"Your punishment exercise?"

Gordon flipping Bennet, thought Norm. Was his mum **ever** going to stop banging on about the punishment exercise? It was flipping Friday! He'd got the whole weekend to do it! In the meantime, Norm would just have to continue putting it off for as long as possible and change the subject whenever he could. Which was why, for once, it actually wasn't **too** annoying at all when Dave suddenly wandered into the kitchen.

"You got a parcel," said Norm.

"What?" said Dave. "Where?"

"There," said Norm with a tilt of his head. "On the table."

"Yesss!" yelled Dave, grabbing the parcel and immediately ripping it open to reveal not only a goalie shirt, but an impressive looking pair of goalie gloves as well.

"Fancy a kick about, Dave?"

Dave turned to his big brother, looking somewhat confused. "What did you say?"

Norm shrugged as nonchalantly as he could. "I just asked if you fancied a kick about, that's all?"

"What? You mean ***now?***"

"Yeah," said Norm.

"But..." began Dave.

"What?" said Norm.

"You hate...I mean, you strongly detest football."

"I do," said Norm. "But I've got a match tomorrow."

"A ***match?***" said Dave. "Really?"

Norm nodded. "Really."

"How come?"

"Just have."

"Brill!" said Dave heading for the stairs. "I'll be out in a minute!"

"That's really great, love," said Norm's mum.

"Seriously?" said Norm.

"Seriously," said Norm's mum. "It's about time you had another interest.

"What do you mean, Mum?"

"I mean, apart from biking."

Great. Thanks a-flipping lot, Mum, thought Norm, suddenly remembering his missing bike. Not that he'd ever actually **forgotten** about it. How **could** he? It would be like forgetting to breathe. And that, thought Norm, was just never **ever** going to happen. Or at least he flipping hoped not, anyway.

"Hi," said Brian, walking into the kitchen.

"Look who it is," muttered Norm. "Nerd of the Rings."

"That's not very nice, love," said Norm's mum as Brian immediately started tucking into the crisps without bothering to ask.

"But..." began Norm.

"What?" said Norm's mum.

Norm sighed. He knew there was no point saying anything. There never flipping was. It was one rule for him – and another for his brothers. Always flipping had been. Always flipping would be.

"You've got a parcel," said Norm.

"What?" said Brian excitedly. "Where?"

"There," said Norm with a tilt of his head.

"Aw, brilliant!" said Brian making a beeline for the table.

Norm, meanwhile had had enough and was making a beeline for the hall.

"I thought you were supposed to be playing football with Dave?" said Norm's mum.

"I am, but I need a pee," said Norm. "Sorry, Mum."

Norm's mum pulled a face. "Why are you sorry? It's perfectly natural."

"Yeah, but I forgot to ask first," said Norm, disappearing out the door.

CHAPTER 20

Norm and Dave hadn't even kicked a ball when the inevitable inevitably happened.

"Hello, **Norman!**" said Chelsea, popping up on the other side of the fence.

"What flipping kept you?" muttered Norm sarcastically.

"I had to change," said Chelsea.

"Uh?"

"Out of my kit, I mean. There's no need for me to change in any **other** way, is there, **Norman?**"

"What?" said Norm.

"I'm perfect just the way I am!" said Chelsea.

Dave laughed.

"Hello, Dave," said Chelsea.

"Hi," grinned Dave.

"Aw, he's sooo cute," said Chelsea in a squeaky baby voice. "Don't you think so, **Norman?**"

"Not really, no," said Norm.

"Aw, don't listen to him, Dave," said Chelsea. "He's only teasing."

"He's flipping not," mumbled Norm.

"It's OK," said Dave. "I'm used to it."

"Well you **shouldn't** be," said Chelsea. "I think he's very mean."

Norm huffed. "Who flipping **cares** what you think?"

"Do you actually want to borrow these, or not?" said Chelsea, holding up a pair of football boots.

Dave laughed and turned to Norm. "Are you borrowing Chelsea's boots?"

"Yeah, so?" said Norm. "What's wrong with that?"

"Yeah, Dave?" said Chelsea. "What **is** wrong with that?"

"Er, nothing," said Dave sheepishly. "Sorry."

"It's OK," laughed Chelsea. "I'm only teasing!"

Right, thought Norm. So it was OK for **other** people to tease his brothers – but not **him?** Flipping typical. He knew he couldn't say anything though. Or rather, he could. But he knew he **shouldn't** say anything. Not if he didn't want to end up playing football in his bare feet the next day, like a flipping medieval kid or something. It was **so** annoying.

"So?" said Chelsea.

"What?" said Norm.

"Do you want them or not?"

"Er, yeah."

Chelsea raised her eyebrows. "What do you say, **Norman?**"

Norm sighed wearily. "Please?"

"Good boy," said Chelsea, clambering over the fence.

Norm was horrified. "What are you doing?"

"What does it look like I'm doing?" said Chelsea. "I'm coming to give them to you."

"But..."

"You got a problem with that?"

Norm thought for a moment. Had he got a problem with that? Flipping right he had. Why couldn't she just have handed them over the flipping fence, or chucked them into the garden? Why did she **always** have to be so unbe-flipping-lievably annoying?

"Well?" said Chelsea. "Have you?"

"Nah," said Norm.

"Good," said Chelsea handing Norm the boots. "Here you go then."

"Thanks."

"Better try them on, just in case."

"Yeah, s'pose so," said Norm sitting down on the grass and taking his trainers off.

"What's the score, by the way?"

"Oh, we're not having a proper game," said Dave. "We're just having a kick about."

"Excellent," said Chelsea. "Can I play?"

Norm opened his mouth to say something but Dave beat him to it.

"Course you can! I'm in goal! Look – I've got a new shirt **and** some special goalie gloves!"

"Cool," said Chelsea. "In that case, let's see if you can stop **this** bad boy!"

Norm watched as Chelsea ran up to the ball and booted it. Dave didn't even move. He didn't have **time** to move as the ball shot straight towards his head. The only reason it didn't actually **hit** his head was because he just managed to stick his hands up and catch it in the nick of time.

"Whoa!" said Dave. "That was **seriously** hard!"

Chelsea laughed. "That was nothing."

"Really?" said Dave incredulously.

"Yeah, really," said Chelsea. "I wasn't even trying."

"I'm not joking, Norm," said Dave. "That was **much** harder than one of **your** shots!"

"Yeah, whatever," said Norm, putting on Chelsea's boots.

"My hands are still **stinging!**" said Dave. "Even **with** the gloves!"

Norm sighed. This was actually beginning to cheese him off. Even though he tried telling himself he wasn't bothered, somewhere deep down inside, he obviously **was**. But why? That was the question. Who **cared** if Chelsea could kick a flipping football harder than he could? So flipping what? He **hated** football! It wasn't like she was better than him at **mountain biking**. Norm could understand being bothered if she was. Yeah, thought Norm. Like **that** was ever going to happen.

"Your turn, **Norman.**"

"What?" said Norm.

"Your shot," said Chelsea.

Norm was puzzled. He might not have known too much about football, but he was pretty sure that players didn't simply take **turns** to shoot. Maybe they did in the olden days, when everyone wore top hats and had tea and cakes at half time. But surely not anymore?

"Come on!" said Chelsea. "We're waiting!"

Gordon flipping Bennet, thought Norm standing up. He might as well just do it and get it over with. And anyway, he could probably do with the practice before the match tomorrow.

"No pressure," said Dave, rolling the ball out to Norm.

Norm stared intently at the ball for a few moments. As if that was somehow going to help. The truth was – as Norm knew only too well – that it would be a minor miracle if he actually made **contact** with the ball, let alone it going anywhere near the goal. OK, so he'd scored the last time he and Dave had played. But that had been a complete and utter fluke. Like the ball hitting him on the head at school and flying into the goal. That had been another fluke. Surely it was too much to expect **three** flukes in a row, thought Norm? Or maybe it **wasn't.** Maybe Norm needed to start thinking a bit more positively. Maybe he **did** actually have some kind of talent for football, no matter how much he disliked it or how much of a waste of time he might think it was. Maybe he...

"Today sometime, **Norman!**" said Chelsea, derailing Norm's train of thought.

Right, thought Norm. This was it. The moment of truth.

"Ready, Dave?"

"He's been ready for the last half an hour!"

laughed Chelsea. "Never mind a new goalie shirt, he's going to need his **pyjamas** at this rate!"

Norm took a deep breath and started to run towards the ball. **He'd** flipping show **her**. She wouldn't be laughing in a...

"AAAAAAARGH!" yelled Norm, treading on his untied laces and flying through the air before landing face first on the grass.

Chelsea promptly burst into hysterics.

"Yeah, very funny," said Norm propping himself up on his elbows.

"Oh, come on!" spluttered Chelsea.

"What?"

"That was **hilarious!**"

"Really?" said Norm. "You think so?"

"Erm, well…" began Dave.

"What?" said Norm irritably.

"It **was** a **bit** hilarious."

"Shut up, Dave!"

"**That's** not very nice, **Norman.**"

Norm sighed. He knew that it was important to at least **try** and keep calm and not show Chelsea just how embarrassed and angry he was really feeling. As it happened he didn't actually **have** to try and keep calm, because at that precise moment there was an unexpected beeping sound from his trousers.

Norm stood up and got his phone out of his pocket. He'd got a Facebook message.

He didn't need to know who the message was from or what it was about. He didn't particularly **care** who it was from or what it was about. All Norm knew was that it was the perfect excuse to disappear back inside and leave Chelsea and Dave to it.

"Where are you going?" said Chelsea, watching Norm as he headed towards the house.

"None of your flipping business," snapped Norm.

"All right, **Norman!**" laughed Chelsea. "Keep your hair on!"

Keep calm, thought Norm. Keep calm and carry on.

CHAPTER 21

The message turned out to be from Connor Wright, checking to see if Norm had made his mind up yet about whether to play football the next day or not. Norm had only just messaged back to say that he **had** made his mind up and that indeed he **would** play when there was a knock on his bedroom door.

Gordon flipping Bennet, thought Norm. Why was it always so flipping hard to get a bit of peace and quiet in this **stupid** little house? All he wanted to do was chill on his iPad for a while. Play some games. Maybe look at a few biking videos. Was that **really** too much to hope for? Apparently so.

There was another knock on the door, only this time slightly more persistent.

"GO AWAY!" yelled Norm. "LEAVE ME ALONE!"

The door opened.

"I said leave me alone, you little—"

"Little what, son?" said Norm's dad, walking into the room.

"Whoa!" said Norm. "Sorry, Dad! Didn't realise it was **you!**"

Norm's dad laughed. "I should hope not!"

"I thought it was Brian!"

"Sorry to disappoint you."

"I'm not disappointed," said Norm.

"Good," said Norm's dad. "What were you doing, anyway?"

Norm shrugged. "Nothing much. Just, you know… stuff?"

"Stuff, eh?"

Norm nodded.

"I hear you're playing football tomorrow."

"What?" said Norm. "Oh, yeah, I am."

"That's strange," said Norm's dad. "You don't even **like** football."

"Yeah, well, you know…" said Norm.

"But then, thinking about it…"

"What, Dad?"

"Well, I mean, it's not like you can go **biking**, is it?"

Norm sighed. Maybe it would have been better if Brian **had** walked through the door after all. At least Brian would have just started banging on about *Lord of the flipping Rings* or whatever instead of immediately reminding Norm about his bike getting nicked! Like Norm actually **needed** reminding! Which reminded Norm – he really ought to post something on Facebook, like Connor Wright had suggested.

"About that," said Norm's dad.

"About what?" said Norm.

"Your **bike**, Norman!"

"Oh, right," said Norm. "What about it?"

"Well, I've just had an interview."

"What?"

"I've just had an interview," said Norm's dad.

"Yeah, but..."

"What's that got to do with your bike?"

Norm nodded.

"Good question," said Norm's dad.

Yeah, thought Norm. It was. So what was the flipping answer?

"The thing is..."

Norm sighed. **What** was the thing? There was always a flipping thing! Why did there even have to **be** a thing? Why couldn't his dad just get on with it? Why couldn't he just get straight to the point instead of always going via the flipping scenic route? Why couldn't he just cut to the chase?

"I think it went pretty well."

"What did?" said Norm. "The interview?"

Norm's dad nodded and smiled. "Well, I know it did."

"So, you mean…"

"Fingers crossed," said Norm's dad crossing his fingers.

Norm wasn't entirely sure how he was expected to react. But it was slowly beginning to dawn on him that whatever it was that his dad was trying to tell him might well be even **better** news than he thought.

"I'm not saying I've **definitely** got the job," said Norm's dad. "But, well…"

Norm waited, desperately trying to resist the urge to put words into his dad's mouth – no matter **how** much he wanted to.

"If I **am** offered it…"

Gordon flipping Bennet, thought Norm. Stop bottom burping around and just flipping **say** it! It was driving him mad!

"We'll soon be able to afford **proper** coco pops again."

Norm stared blankly at his dad. Had he heard him right? Coco pops? Was that **really** what this was all about? After all that build up and all that waffle? Coco pops? Not that there was anything wrong with coco pops, thought Norm. Far from it in fact. There was **nothing** wrong with coco pops. Nothing at all. Especially **proper** coco pops. That wasn't the point. The point was – this wasn't exactly the news that Norm had been hoping for. His dad had led him up the garden path – and then just flipping **left** him there!

"Well, Norman? What do you think?"

"Erm, that's great, Dad. But...."

"What?" grinned Norm's dad.

Norm took a deep breath. He was just going to have to come right out with it and say it.

"What about my bike?"

"Your bike?"

Norm nodded.

"I'll just buy you a new one."

"Pardon?" said Norm.

"I'll buy you a new one," said Norm's dad airily. "Sorry. Should've said."

For a few moments Norm didn't know whether to laugh or cry. In the end he did neither and just continued to stare at his dad instead.

"Aren't you going to say something?"

"Thanks?" croaked Norm.

"You're welcome," said Norm's dad. "Actually it's the least I can do."

"Uh?" croaked Norm.

"Well let's face it, it was **my** fault your old bike wasn't insured."

True, thought Norm. It **was** his dad's fault, come to think of it. And how weird, hearing his bike referred to as **old**. But it really **was** now. His bike was gone. It was toast. Ancient history. Who cared what had happened to it? Norm certainly didn't. Not anymore, anyway. All Norm cared about now was that he was going to get a brand spanking **new** one. And it wouldn't just be any old bike either. Oh no. It was going to be the very latest, state of the art, most awesome, all singing, all dancing best flipping bike his dad's money could buy! There'd be no excuse now for Norm not becoming World Mountain Biking Champion one day. None whatso-flipping-ever!

"But like I said, Norman. I haven't **definitely** got the job. So don't say anything to anyone just yet.

And don't go building your hopes up **too** much."

But Norm didn't reply. He was already looking up new bikes on his iPad.

"Norman?"

"Uh? What?" said Norm distractedly.

"I said don't go building up your hopes **too** much, will you?"

"Sorry? What? No, course not, Dad."

"Right, well I'd better leave you to it, then," said Norm's dad heading for the door.

"Er, Dad?"

"Yes?" said Norm's dad, stopping and turning around.

"Erm, when do you think you might hear about the job?" said Norm. "You know? For sure?"

"Soon, hopefully," said Norm's dad, setting off again.

Norm sighed. Soon? What was **that** supposed to mean? How soon was flipping **soon**? Tomorrow? The day after? The day **after** the day after? One thing was for sure. Whenever soon was, it wasn't flipping soon **enough**.

"Tea time, love!" called Norm's mum from the foot of the stairs.

"Be down in a minute, Mum!" yelled Norm, immediately clicking on a particularly cool and particularly **expensive**-looking bike.

CHAPTER 22

"Norman?"

"What?" yawned
Norm.

"You awake?"

It was a good question, thought Norm. **Was** he awake? He couldn't actually remember going to sleep in the first place. All he could remember was looking at new bikes on his iPad.

"What time's the match?"

Norm opened his eyes to find his dad looking at him from the end of the bed.

"What match?"

"What do you mean, what match?" said Norm's dad. "The one you're **playing** in!"

Norm groaned as he suddenly remembered. He didn't even **have** to play in this stupid football match now. It didn't actually matter whether Connor Wright knew a guy who knew a guy who might know a guy who might know something about his bike or whatever. Except that come to think of it he **did** actually have to play because he'd gone and flipping well told Grandpa he would! What did he have to go and do **that** for? Well, apart from the fact that Grandpa had pretty much told him he was about to pop his clogs any minute and that it would make him **happy** if Norm played? But apart from **that**.

"Well?" said Norm's dad.

"'Snot till Saturday, Dad," mumbled Norm.

"Pardon?" said Norm's dad irritably.

Norm sighed. "It's not till **Saturday**."

"Norman?"

"Yeah?"

"It **is** Saturday."

"It **is?**" said Norm. "Whoa."

"What time do you have to be at school?"

"Half nine, I think."

"In that case, you'd better get a move on!"

"What? Why?" said Norm.

"It's twenty past nine **now**, Norman!" said Norm's dad heading for the door. "Get downstairs as quick as you can!"

"'Kay, Dad," said Norm wearily, rolling out of bed and following.

Norm's dad suddenly stopped and turned around. "Where do you think you're going?"

Norm pulled a face. What kind of stupid question was **that?** Wasn't it flipping **obvious** where he was

going? Downstairs!

"Get dressed first!" said Norm's dad, setting off, the vein on the side of his head beginning to throb slightly.

"Gordon flipping Bennet," muttered Norm. "Make your mind up."

"What was that?" yelled Norm's dad from halfway down the stairs.

"Er, I said I'll be down in a sec, Dad!" said Norm as his phone beeped.

Eventually locating his phone beneath yesterday's discarded pair of pants, Norm looked at it and saw that it was a message from Mikey.

"orite?"

"Alrite," Norm messaged back.

266

"u playing futbal?"

"yeh worse flipping luck," wrote Norm, his fingers a blur, before hitting send.

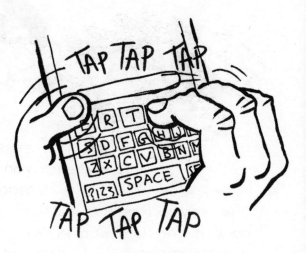

"**wot time?**" said Mikey.

"Now," fired back Norm, chucking his phone down again and throwing some clothes on in double-quick time. Not that *that* was saying very much. Norm was unlikely to ever win any prizes for speed-dressing, in the even *unlikelier* event that he should ever actually enter a speed-dressing competition in the first place.

"You ready yet, love?" yelled Norm's mum from the hall.

"Coming, Mum!" shouted Norm, by now sauntering along the landing with all the urgency of a slug.

"HURRY UP, NORMAN!" screamed Brian and Dave, heading out the front door.

"Yes, hurry up, Norman," said Norm's dad rattling his car keys. "We don't want to be late!"

Norm stopped at the top of the stairs and stared. This couldn't be happening, could it? It certainly **shouldn't** be happening. And if Norm had anything to do with it, it flipping well **wouldn't** be happening!

"What's the matter, love?" said his mum.

"Did you say...**we**, Dad?"

Norm's dad nodded. "Uh-huh."

"As in..."

"As in all of us," said Norm's dad nodding again. "Uh-huh."

"But…"

Norm's mum smiled. "What's wrong with *that*, love? We thought you'd like us there, cheering you on!"

"I might even *sing*," said Norm's dad.

Gordon flipping Bennet, thought Norm. This was rapidly going from bad to worse. In fact, never mind going from bad to worse – it was going from frankly **_horrific_**, to worst flipping nightmare ever! In fact, never mind **_going_** – it had already flipping **_gone!_**

"Well?" said Norm's dad with another rattle of his car keys. "Are you coming, or what?"

Norm sighed. "Do I have a choice?"

"Not really, no!" said Norm's dad heading out the door.

"Come on, love!" said Norm's mum cheerily. "What's the worst that could happen?"

Norm thought for a moment. What **_was_** the worst that could possibly happen?

"Hurry up, **_Norman!_**" said an instantly recognisable voice outside. "We're waiting!"

Ah, thought Norm. That was it. **_That_** was the worst thing that could happen. And it looked like it just flipping had.

CHAPTER 23

Norm remained silent the whole journey. Partly because he was still so shocked and traumatised and couldn't quite believe what was happening – and partly because he couldn't have got a word in edgeways even if he **had** wanted to say something. Everybody else was talking nonstop. Seemingly **all** at the same time. Even John felt compelled to provide a running commentary on everything he could see out the window, yapping and barking for all he was worth, like he'd never been outside before.

YAP YAP YAP

271

The only consolation as far as Norm was concerned – and it was a pretty **small** consolation – was that the journey from his house to the school only took a few minutes. Even so, to Norm, they seemed like the longest few minutes of his entire life. Being stuck in a car with his brothers was one thing – but being stuck in a car with his brothers **and** Chelsea? That was pure torture. As for Chelsea coming to watch him actually play in the match, as **well** as his entire flipping family? Norm shuddered to even **think** what **that** was going to be like.

Of course, there was always the possibility that it could all be part of some elaborate practical joke and that they were merely **pretending** they were going to the match when in fact they were just going to drop him off and go to IKEA instead? It was unlikely though, thought Norm. And anyway, why would Chelsea go to IKEA with the rest of his family? Then again, why would **anyone** go to IKEA full flipping stop?

"Here, love. Take this," said Norm's mum from the front seat, turning around and shoving a banana under Norm's nose. Or, at least, that was the plan, before Norm's dad braked a little too sharply as they arrived at the school, causing Norm's mum to very nearly shove the banana **up** Norm's nose instead.

"Well, that's **one** way of getting your five a day I suppose!" laughed Chelsea, prompting Brian and Dave to burst out laughing too.

"Shut up!" hissed Norm through gritted teeth.

"**That's** not very nice, Norman," said Norm's dad. "Say sorry."

"Sorry, Dad," said Norm.

"Not to **me!** To Chelsea!"

Norm sighed. "Sorry."

"That's OK," grinned Chelsea. "I'll put it down to pre-match nerves."

"Whatever," muttered Norm.

"Come on, love. Eat up, now," said Norm's mum. "You haven't had breakfast."

Norm shrugged. "Not bothered."

"It'll give you *energy*."

Norm pulled a face. What did he need flipping energy for? He had no intention of running around the football pitch any more than was strictly necessary. The only thing he was actually going to need energy for, was riding the brand new bike he was going to be getting sooner or later. Preferably sooner.

"Let's go," said Norm's dad, opening his door and getting out of the car.

Norm sat perfectly still, whilst everyone else got

out the car and began making their way to the football pitch.

"That includes you too, Norman."

Norm took a deep breath and got out. There was no point delaying it any longer. He was just going to have to get it over and....

"MIND OUT, NORM!" yelled Mikey, jamming on his brakes and skidding to a halt.

Norm knew an opportunity when he saw one and immediately collapsed to the ground like a ton of bricks, rolling and writhing around clutching his leg, like he'd seen footballers on the television doing.

"Aaaaaaaagh!" moaned Norm. "I'm in agony! I think my leg's broken!"

Mikey pulled a face. "But I never touched you!"

"Shut up, Mikey!" hissed Norm out the corner of his mouth.

"Very funny, son," laughed Norm's dad. "Up you get, now."

Looking daggers at his best friend, Norm got to his feet again and began trudging slowly after the others.

"Thanks **very** much, Mikey. What are **you** doing here, anyway?"

"I've come to watch **you!**" said Mikey. "Thought you might appreciate a bit of support!"

Norm sighed wearily. "Thanks."

Mikey looked rather puzzled. "You don't seem very happy, Norm."

"What?" said Norm. "No, I'm ecstatic. Really I am."

"Hey, guys!" said a voice.

Norm and Mikey stopped and swivelled around to see Connor Wright heading towards them.

"All set, Norman?"

Norm shrugged. "S'pose."

"Great," said Connor Wright. "I want you to play up front."

Uh? thought Norm. And what exactly was *that* supposed to flipping mean?

"I'll be on the right. Hopefully whip a few balls in for you to get your head on!"

A *few* balls? thought Norm. How many were they going to be playing with? As for getting his *head* on any of them? Connor Wright could dream on!

"All right, Connor?" said another voice.

Norm turned to see a kid from one of the other classes approaching. He didn't know him. All he knew was that he had some kind of weird name, like Squid, or Sponge or something.

Connor Wright looked surprised. "What are you doing here, Shark?"

Shark, thought Norm. That was it.

"I've come to play," said Shark.

"But I thought you said you weren't going to be able to make it?"

"Yeah, well we were supposed to be going away for the weekend," said Shark. "But we're not anymore, so here I am."

"You left it a bit *late*, didn't you?" said Connor Wright.

"Yeah, well, there was something I needed to do on the way," said Shark, hopping from one foot to another.

Norm was trying not to get *too* excited. If Connor Wright hadn't been *expecting* Shark to turn up did that mean that *he* was Shark's replacement?

Because if so...

"Well, this is a bit awkward," said Connor Wright.

"What is?" said Norm.

"Well, I thought we were going to be a man short. But it turns out we're not."

"I see," said Norm. "So does that mean you don't actually **need** me now?"

Connor Wright nodded sheepishly. "Erm, well, 'fraid so."

By now Norm had completely given up trying not to get too excited. Not that he was allowing himself to **show** it. That wouldn't be cool at all. But **inside**, he was dancing for joy. Which was unusual for a start, because Norm hated dancing almost as much as he hated football.

"I'm really sorry, Norman," said Connor Wright.

"It's OK," said Norm as casually as possible. "I don't actually **need** you to have a word with anyone about my bike anymore, anyway."

"Oh, I already did," said Connor Wright. "But it doesn't matter."

"Hang on," said Shark, still hopping about. "**You're** Norman?"

"What?" said Norm.

"**You're** Norman?" said Shark. "The guy with the bike?"

"Yeah," said Norm. "Why?"

"Er, nothing," said Shark, exchanging a quick glance with Connor Wright. "Just wondered, that's all."

"Come on then," said Connor Wright, hurrying Shark away. "We'd better go and get changed."

"'Kay," said Shark following him. "I'm sorry, Norman."

Uh? thought Norm. What was *he* sorry for? By turning up when he had, he'd actually done Norm a massive favour! He'd got abso-flipping-lutely *nothing* to apologise for, as far as Norm was concerned! Norm actually owed this guy *big* time!

"You know why they call him Shark, don't you?" said Mikey.

"No, why?" said Norm.

"You haven't noticed, then?"

"Noticed what?" said Norm. "He's got a fin on his back?"

"No," chuckled Mikey.

"His diet consists mainly of seals?"

Mikey burst out laughing.

"What then?" said Norm.

"He never stops moving!" said Mikey.

"What?" said Norm. "Oh right. I just thought he needed the toilet."

"That was out of order."

Norm pulled a face. "What was? The toilet?"

"No," said Mikey. "The way he just turned up and all of a sudden he's straight back in the team and you're out? I just don't think that's **right**, Norm."

"Yeah, well I couldn't care less," said Norm. "I'm getting a new bike!"

"Whoa! Seriously?" said Mikey.

"Seriously," said Norm.

"Aw, that's **brilliant**, Norm!"

"You're not flipping kidding!" said Norm.

"How come?" said Mikey.

"Uh?" said Norm. "How come I'm not kidding?"

"No!" said Mikey. "How come you're getting a new bike?

"My dad's got a job."

"No, he hasn't."

Norm spun round to see his dad walking towards him, checking his phone for messages.

"What?" spluttered Norm. "But what about my bike, Dad? You said..."

"Is that **really** all you can think about?" said Norm's dad, the vein on the side of his head beginning to throb ever so slightly. "Your **bike?**"

"Erm, well..."

Norm's dad sighed. "You know I've got a good mind to make you **walk** home, Norman?"

"Promise?" muttered Norm.

"What was that?"

"Nothing, Dad," said Norm.

"Hello, Mikey, by the way," said Norm's dad.

"Hi," said Mikey. "Sorry about the job."

Norm's dad smiled. "No need to be sorry, Mikey."

"But..." began Mikey.

"If he'd actually let me **finish,**" said Norm's dad, looking pointedly in Norm's direction, "what I was **going** to say was that I haven't heard back yet."

"**Yet?**" said Norm.

Norm's dad nodded.

"So you still might get the job?"

"Fingers crossed. Yes, Norman. I still might get it."

Norm breathed an enormous sigh of relief.

"Now hurry up and get changed," said Norm's dad."

"There's no need," said Norm.

Norm's dad pulled a face. "What do you mean, there's no need? Of course you need to change. You can't play football dressed like that!"

"That's the thing," said Norm.

"What's the thing?"

Norm grinned. "I'm not playing."

CHAPTER 24

Norm couldn't **wait** to get home. The past few minutes had been such an emotional roller coaster, for a while he honestly thought he was going to throw up. From thinking he was playing football one minute, to finding out that he wasn't the next 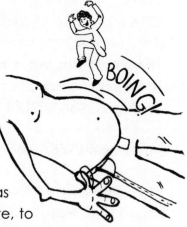 – to **thinking** he wasn't getting a new bike after all and then realising that he still might – it felt like someone was using his stomach as a trampoline. Now all Norm wanted was to be left alone in his room, with only his iPad for company. No more droning parents. No more squabbling brothers. No more yapping dogs. And **definitely** no more annoying occasional next door neighbours.

Nothing. Zilch. *Nada*. Thank you and goodnight.

"Well, that was a shame, wasn't it?" said Norm's mum as the car pulled into the street.

"What was?" said Norm's dad. "Norman not playing football?"

"Yes, I was looking forward to it," said Norm's mum. "Oh well, there's always next time, I suppose."

No there flipping ***isn't***, thought Norm. He'd been blackmailed once already. There was no flipping way it was ***ever*** happening again.

"I was looking forward to it, as well, actually!" piped up Chelsea.

"Aw, were you, Chelsea?" said Norm's mum.

"Yeah," said Chelsea. "I could've done with a good laugh!"

Brian and Dave both burst into hysterics. Even Norm's parents seemed to find it quite funny. But Norm wasn't listening. Something had just caught his eye as he stared out the window. Something that looked strangely familiar. It couldn't be? Could it? Surely not? It flipping **was!** But...

"Is that your bike, love?" said Norm's mum spotting the same something that Norm had spotted.

"Er, yeah, it is, Mum," said Norm.

"Where?" said Norm's dad.

"There," said Norm's mum. "Leaning on the fence?"

"So it is," said Norm's dad, slowing down and stopping outside the house. "What a stroke of luck! Well, for me, anyway. Maybe not so much for you, Norman."

"What?" said Norm.

"Well there's no need to buy you a new one now, is there?"

Norm **tried** to say something, but the words somehow got stuck in his throat. He'd frequently felt gobsmacked before – but never quite **this** gobsmacked. This was taking gobsmacked to a whole new level.

"How did it get there?" said Brian.

"Someone cycled it there, you doughnut!" said Dave.

"Yes, but who?" said Brian.

"I dunno," said Dave. "Whoever took it in the first place, I suppose."

Brian sighed. "Yes, but who took it in the first place?"

"Grandpa!" squealed Dave excitedly.

"What are you **talking** about, Dave?" said Brian. "Why on earth would **Grandpa** take Norman's bike?"

"What?" said Dave. "No, I mean, look! Grandpa!"

Norm looked. Sure enough, Grandpa was ambling down the street towards them.

"Hello, Dad," said Norm's mum, getting out of the car. "Cup of tea?"

"I thought you'd never ask!" said Grandpa as everybody else got out of the car, too.

"Yeah! Grandpa!" yelled Brian and Dave, spilling onto the pavement and immediately swarming round Grandpa, each vying for his attention.

"Clear off, you two!" said Grandpa pretending to swat them away as if they were a couple of flies. "I want a word with your big brother. Alone."

"What is it, Grandpa?" said Norm once everyone had gone inside and Chelsea had thankfully disappeared next door.

"How was it?"

Norm pulled a face. "How was what?"

"The match?"

"Oh, right," said Norm. "I've no idea."

"What do you *mean*, you've no idea?" said Grandpa, his cloud-like eyebrows meeting in the middle.

"I didn't play."

"Oh, I see."

Norm looked at Grandpa for a moment before suddenly remembering what Grandpa had told him. About not playing football once when **he** was young and the feelings of regret he'd had ever since.

"Sorry, Grandpa."

"Eh, what?" said Grandpa. "What for?"

"For not making you happy?"

Grandpa's eyes crinkled ever so slightly in the corners. "You didn't actually **believe** all that guff, did you, Norman?"

Norm looked puzzled. "You mean..."

"I made it all up," said Grandpa.

"What?" said Norm.

"I can't believe you actually **fell** for it."

Norm sighed. So it was all a wind-up? **He** couldn't believe he'd actually fallen for it, either!

"Is that your bike, by the way?" said Grandpa.

Norm nodded.

"Thought so. Where did you find it?"

"Right there," said Norm.

"Pardon?" said Grandpa.

"Someone left it there while we were out."

"Who?"

Norm thought for a moment. The penny didn't exactly **drop** – but it was definitely getting **much** closer to the edge. All it needed now was a little shove. Maybe the reason Shark had turned up so late for the match was because he had to return the bike first! He said there was something he needed to do, didn't he? Maybe **that** was what he'd needed to do! Maybe that was why he'd asked Norm if he was the guy with the bike! Maybe that was why he'd said sorry! He was apologising for taking it! Or **borrowing** it or whatever. That wasn't the point. The point was, maybe, just maybe, when Connor Wright had had a word with a guy who knew a guy who knew someone who might know something about his bike – **that** guy was Shark!

"Well?" said Grandpa. "Who was it?"

Norm shrugged. "Just this guy."

"Hmm," said Grandpa. "You don't seem very **happy** about it?"

"What?" said Norm.

"You've got your **bike** back, Norman!" said Grandpa. "I thought you'd be over the moon!"

Over the moon?
thought Norm.
Under a flipping
cloud more like. A
big, black storm
cloud with flipping
knobs on.

"Don't forget your
punishment exercise, love!"
called Norm's mum from the
front door.

"Gordon flipping Bennet,"
muttered Norm.

"Cheer up," said Grandpa. "It
might never happen."

Norm sighed. It just flipping **had**.

"Hilarious stuff from one
of my comic heroes!"
Harry Hill

Don't miss Norm's next hilarious adventure...

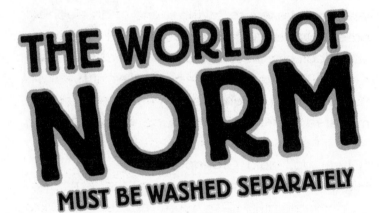

THE WORLD OF
NORM
MUST BE WASHED SEPARATELY

COMING OCTOBER 2014!

Read on for a sneak peek...

ORCHARD BOOKS
www.orchardbooks.co.uk

CHAPTER 1

Norm knew it was going to be one of those days when he was woken by the sound of an elephant breaking wind in the next room. Or at least that's what it sounded like to Norm. Not that Norm had ever actually heard an elephant breaking wind in the next room before – or anywhere else for that matter – but if he ever did, he imagined that's what it would probably sound like.

Then again, thought Norm, you only had to close a door in this stupid little house and it sounded like the flipping world was about to end. So actually, thinking about it – thought Norm, thinking about it – it might not have been an elephant breaking wind after all. It could have been just about anything. It could've been his dad breaking wind. Or his mum for that matter. Maybe his mum and dad had broken wind at exactly the same time? Maybe that's what couples ended up doing when they'd been together for as long as his parents had. Their digestive systems somehow synchronised and they ended up doing just about everything at the same time.

Norm shuddered. What on earth was he doing, thinking about his parents' bodily functions at this time on a Sunday morning? Frankly, thought Norm, he had no particular wish to think about his parents' bodily functions at any time, let alone before he'd even got out of bed. And especially before he'd even had breakfast.

"Norm!" yelled a distant, muffled-sounding voice.

Funny, thought Norm propping himself up on one elbow and looking around. Where was that coming from? Because there was only one person who ever called him Norm.

"Mikey?" said Norm getting out of bed. "Where are you?"

Read
MUST BE WASHED SEPARATELY
to find out what happens next!

COMING SOON!

Want more Norm? Then you'll love this flipping brilliant Norm-themed activity book!

Packed with loads of great Norm facts, pant-wettingly-hilarious jokes and crazy doodle activities!

For a sneak peek of what to expect, read on...

Norm's Vital Statistics

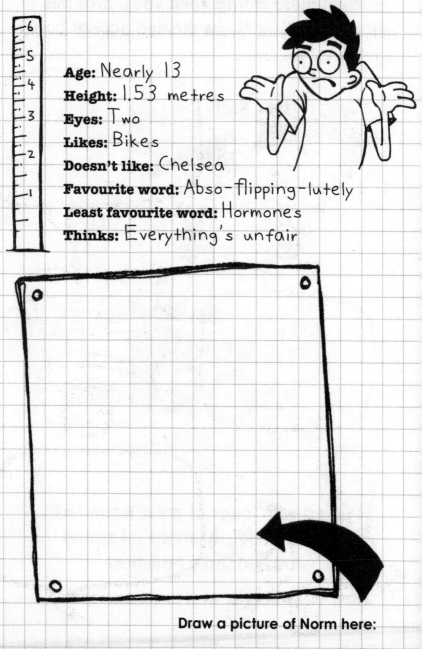

Age: Nearly 13
Height: 1.53 metres
Eyes: Two
Likes: Bikes
Doesn't like: Chelsea
Favourite word: Abso-flipping-lutely
Least favourite word: Hormones
Thinks: Everything's unfair

Draw a picture of Norm here:

Just Flipping Say It

Fill in the bubbles with questions, statements or anything else you feel like saying.

Barmy Bike Jokes

Why can't a bike stand up on its own?
Because it's two-tyred
(too tired, geddit?)

What's the hardest thing about learning to ride a bike?
The pavement.

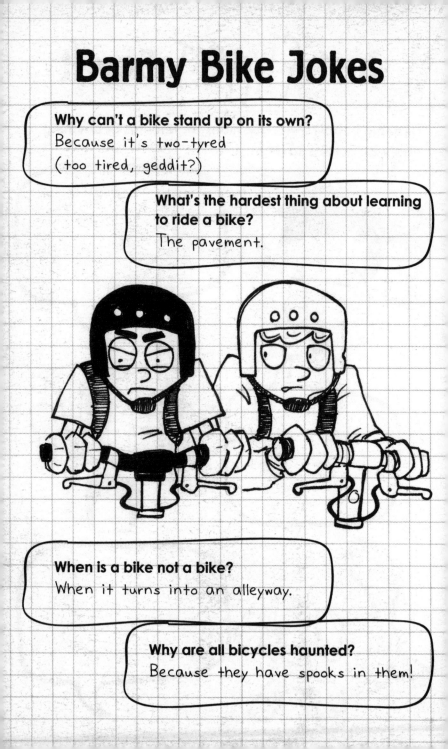

When is a bike not a bike?
When it turns into an alleyway.

Why are all bicycles haunted?
Because they have spooks in them!